Table of Contents

Chapter 1

He finished buttoning up his crisp, white dress shirt but left the top buttons undone, exposing the smooth tan skin of his throat.

"Ready to go?" Liam asked, his voice thick with desire as he looked at his wife. Dressed in a gorgeous full-skirted dress and a pearl-string necklace, Josie cut quite a striking figure. They both loved getting dressed for these occasions.

Josie gave him a suggestive wink, "Always."

As she brushed past him, Josie deliberately squeezed the bulge in his pants.

***

The entranceway was decorated in muted colors. Liam and Josie shrugged off their coats and carefully handed them to one of the supervisors who carefully transferred them to the closet.

"Evening, Chelsey. How are you tonight?" Josie asked. The question was standard and had an underlying purpose: They needed to know if there were any potential troublemakers in the house today. Not everybody played well together.

"Good to see you two again," Chelsey glanced through the doorway to her left. "Brandon is in here tonight. I'm on coffee duty." As she said that a pair came out from where Chelsey had been motioning. The man was dressed in a beautiful navy blue suit and a crisp, white button-up. He was holding the hand of his Little, dressed in a yellow dress and holding a penguin stuffie under her arm, nodding as she talked animatedly. He nodded a greeting to Liam and sent a silent signal to Chelsey.

The three of them quietly disappeared into an adjoining room where they could hear cups being prepared.

Liam and Josie stepped through the door, glancing around, greeting some of the other Daddies and Mommies they had come to know outside of this space. Josie kissed his hand, and he watched her disappear around the corner. She would go around the house, greeting everyone before finding somewhere to settle in.

It usually took Liam a while longer to get into the right headspace. Sometimes even longer if he had had a bad day in court, and today had been a *really* bad day. The opposition had put up a really strong defense, and the potential to lose his case was weighing heavily on him. Liam rarely lost, and the threat put him on edge. The anger wasn't welcome here, so he needed a moment to reset. Liam turned around and went through the door where the other couple and Chelsey disappeared a few heartbeats earlier.

The kitchen was set up to be the neutral space. Nothing but coffee happened in there. You could walk in, grab a cup, and sit down. Even if that was all you did all night, it was a safe place, and the people were kind enough to pass no judgments. Chelsey had prepared a fresh pot of coffee and brought a cup over to where he sat on an ancient, wooden kitchen chair.

"Want to talk about it?" Chelsey prompted after passing him the tray with cream and sugar.

"Nah. Thanks, though, Chels. I appreciate the offer." Liam stirred absent-mindedly and listened to the couple as they talked about mundane things, drinking their coffee, and accepting Chelsey's offer of cookies. Liam drained his coffee, savoring the sweet, creamy residue at the bottom of the cup. He ran his hands through his hair and decided to head deeper into the house. Liam did what he always did and stood in the doorway of one of the Little room where a few little girls were coloring and laughing. He loved seeing them as happy as they were. Relaxed and content.

A few girls were wearing onesies, while others wore dresses and bows. The color alone made his heart swell. When he stepped inside, the girls looked up at him. One little girl with a large pink scrunchie holding her long dark hair tied above her head beamed a smile at him, waving ecstatically.

Liam went over and sat down next to her, "Hi, Ella, what are you working on today?"

"It's my favorite!" Ella held up her picture proudly. The page was full of butterflies, colored with every color imaginable. She had even signed her name in the bottom corner of the page.

"That's really good, angel. Can you draw something for me, too?" Liam asked.

Ella immediately complied and pulled out a blank sheet of paper.

When she was done, Liam carefully took the picture from Ella and held it up for inspection.

Good girl! This picture is absolutely beautiful." She beamed at him, and a flush crept up her neck and onto her cheeks.

"Thank you, Mr. Liam," Ella said shyly.

"Can I keep this one?"

Ella nodded and returned to her drawings.

"Thank you, Ella. Be a good little girl, okay?"

"I will, Mr. Liam."

With a gentle pat of her hand, Liam rose to his feet

and left her to her own devices.

It was normal that some Littles would prefer to be in their little space simply. Coloring, snuggling, and doing Little things. Just like anyone else wouldn't always be in the mood for anything more serious than light petting, each Little had their own needs that changed from day to day and from moment to moment.

Liam passed Brandon as he wandered further into the house, who simply acknowledged his existence with a brief nod of his head before continuing his rotation. There were three supervisors throughout the house, aside from Chelsey. While nothing untoward happened, their existence was to ensure the safety and comfort of the people involved. Rules were in place for a reason, and newcomers weren't allowed to be part of the events if they did not agree to all of them.

From somewhere down the hall, Liam heard squeals of joy and hysterical laughter. He knew without needing to go see that it was one of the more salacious rooms. One he liked visiting himself; however, that particular experience would be saved for another time.

Liam found Josie on the couch with a Little snuggled up to her as they watched cartoons on a massive TV hanging on the opposite wall. Josie caught his eye and motioned for him to come over.

Liam gave Josie a kiss on the top of her head and whispered in her ear, "When you're ready, you know where to find me, Jo."

His voice was husky, and Josie felt heat pool between her legs. With Dylan snuggled so close to her, she could feel the muscles in his body tense and relax as he shifted to get more comfortable.

Josie knew Liam had already left. He didn't need an answer. She knew where to find him if she wanted to join him. Right now, she felt content and happy, holding Dylan close to her. While she didn't have her own Little, Dylan was more than eager to share himself with her whenever he could.

"Mommy?"

"Yes, little man?"

"Do you have to go with Mr. Liam now?"

Josie smiled and brushed the hair from his eyes, kissing the tip of his nose, "Of course not, sweetie. We don't have to go anywhere or do anything that you don't want to, remember?"

Dylan nodded and was quiet for a while, his attention on the purple dog on the TV screen. After a short while, he looked up at Josie, "Mommy?"

"Yes, sweetie?"

"Do you think Mr. Liam will want to be my Daddy tonight?"

It took Josie by surprise, and perhaps it showed on her face because Dylan scrunched his face up and hastily added, "It's okay if he doesn't. It's okay if you don't either, Mommy. I just-"

Josie put a gentle finger to his lips, still showing no sign of anger or irritability, "We can go ask him, Dylan. Are you sure that's what you want?"

Josie was serious. She had never seen Dylan interested in anyone other than a handful of other Mommies, and he seemed especially withdrawn from Liam and the other Daddies that frequented the play parties.

"You're not mad at me?" Dylan asked, a catch in his voice.

"Of course not," Josie planted soft kisses all over his face, making him giggle. "You're my sweet baby boy, how could I ever be mad at you?"

Dylan hopped off the couch excitedly, holding Josie's hand, "Can we go now, Mommy?"

"What's the magic word?"

"Please," Dylan laughed and bounced on the balls of his feet, dragging Josie behind him.

As they entered the hallway, Josie gently pulled him to a stop, "Remember, there are other people here too, so we need to be quiet and respectful."

"Yes, Mommy."

The pair made their way through the house. Some doors were closed, and Josie heard the unmistakable sounds of sex coming from them. Behind another, the sharp crack as a paddle met bare flesh. The sounds made Josie lick her lips in anticipation.

They passed by a room that held four "cubicles," which were small safe spaces enclosed with heavy drapes hanging from the ceiling. The curtains were there if the Caregiver and Little needed a little privacy for their aftercare. Not everyone liked to be watched during such an intimate moment. The room was empty for now but would have occupants soon enough.

She felt Dylan hesitate as they neared the room in the back where Liam was sure to be. Josie stopped and pulled him to her, "You really don't have to do anything you don't want to, little man."

"I'm scared you'll be mad and never want to be my Mommy again."

Josie looked at him, reassuringly, "I promised that I would never lie to you, Dylan. And you promised me, too."

Dylan looked at the floor and in the softest voice, said, "I- I don't think I'm ready for that yet."

"It really is okay, Dylan," Josie stressed his name so he would look up at her. "We can go back and just snuggle on the couch exactly like we always do."

"Yes, please." Josie hugged him tightly and

led him back to the TV room, "You don't ever have to do anything you don't want to."

Dylan nodded and looked at the floor as he hesitated in the doorway, his fingers still wrapped around hers, "Is it okay if I watch by myself for a little bit?"

"Whatever you want, little one."

Dylan's mood instantly picked up again, and he leaped into her arms for a hug.

Josie gave Dylan one last big bear hug and helped him get comfortable on the sofa. She handed him his sippy cup and watched from the doorway as he settled himself in.

Josie was a bit disappointed, but she never wanted Dylan to do anything he wasn't ready for, so she didn't get angry. Josie accepted him for who he was and let him do what he needed. It was the same for everyone here. On the odd occasion, they would encounter a bad apple who soured the mood and experience for everyone, but the problems were resolved quickly and quietly.

The rules were there for a reason. No is no; no

exceptions.

Josie hummed to herself as she walked back to the drawing-room, needing to spend a little time with the girls before finding Liam.

"Josie!" an ear-splitting squeal of delight drew her attention to the doorway where a familiar face was impatiently handing off her coat and bag.

"Piper, sweetheart, how have you been?" Josie half-laughed as Piper ran up and nearly knocked her over as she threw her arms around Josie. A full head shorter than Josie, Piper's thin frame and large blue eyes made her look like a doll.

"Everything has been so much fun, Mommy!"

Josie couldn't stop smiling. Piper's laugh was infectious, and her bubbly personality lit up the room. The other Littles stared at her, giggling and whispering. Some even temporarily abandoned their artwork and clumped around the two of them. Piper made friends easily, and she adored the girls as much as they adored her.

***

Liam growled low in his throat, "Just like that, good girl Lexi."

It was one of the rare rooms that had their door open, given the explicit nature of what was happening within. There were two women at Liam's feet, still fully clothed, looking up at him expectantly. He had stripped naked for the scene, the muscles in his thighs working as he shifted his weight as the girls continued their instruction.

The one he called Lexi had a dark green training collar around her neck, and the lead was wrapped around Liam's muscular forearm. Lexi's full-time Daddy, Carlisle, was standing slightly to one side, watching the scene before him. He caught Josie's attention, and she quietly went in, Piper following close behind, her eyes locked on Liam's cock as the girls licked and suckled him.

Josie recognized the other Little as Octavia. She

didn't belong to anyone but, much like a lot of the girls at the party, preferred to have more than one Daddy. She generally went with what she felt in the mood for that day and fell in where they accepted her.

Carlisle motioned Josie over and whispered in her ear, "Liam's a good teacher. I have trained a lot of Littles, but he has that, special touch." Josie couldn't help but notice the bulge in his jeans as his eyes darkened, watching as Liam carefully pulled Lexi closer by the lead, repositioning her for the next lesson.

Josie agreed with Carlisle; Liam was gentle and caring even when training and dealing with extremely bratty, little girls. She knew he secretly liked the fire in their eyes when they tried to defy him.

Josie's eyes wandered around the room and saw that there were a few other people also enjoying the scene. She desperately wanted to join in, especially since Piper was pressing herself against Josie in a way that made her acutely aware that she definitely wasn't a little girl underneath all those frills.

Liam glanced at Josie and Piper and held out his free hand to them. He glanced down at the two in front of him, and they gave the most imperceptible of nods, consenting to the addition of two more to their group. Liam had made arrangements with Carlisle before they had started, and he had agreed to the addition.

Liam stood back, releasing the slack on the lead, and Lexi stood up demurely. She couldn't help but glance at Carlisle as he watched from the sidelines, an action Liam did not miss.

"Octavia, could you help Daddy undress, Lexi, please?"

"Yes, Daddy."

As Josie joined them, she beckoned to Piper, "Come here, pumpkin."

"But-"

The look Josie gave Piper stopped the words in her throat. She gave one lustful glance to Liam and walked into Josie's open arms, "I'm sorry,

Mommy."

"You will get your turn, pumpkin. Daddy is busy teaching a new baby girl the rules."

"Did she talk back?" Piper asked, eyes wide, still watching the scene.

As Octavia unzipped Lexi's summer dress, they watched it fall to the floor. Her bottom was already a little red from where Liam had spanked her.

"Why don't you ask her, Piper?"

Piper bit her lip as did as instructed, "Little Lexi, why is Daddy punishing you?"

Her face flushed red, Lexi looked up at Piper, "I called Daddy a bad word. I'm not allowed to say bad words."

Liam had Lexi positioned on her knees in front of him, her bottom facing him. His cock jerked, but he knew she was not to be touched in that way. Those were the terms set by Carlisle. Liam pulled back his hand and with a loud *whack,* made contact with her bare skin. Lexi squirmed and let out a small sound.

"What are the rules Carlisle has given you,

Lexi?" Liam asked, his voice was hard but still gentle as he addressed her.

"I will not lie."

Whack.

"I will not backtalk or argue."

Whack.

"I will not use bad language."

Whack.

"I will do my chores."

Whack.

Liam softly rubbed over the stinging parts of her flesh, and Lexi let out a moan of pleasure. Her lips were swollen and moist.

Josie had discarded her dress, revealing her bare skin underneath. She enjoyed the thrill of going out into public with the added risk of exposing herself. It made her feel more powerful in a way.

"Kneel for me, please, pumpkin."

Piper thought about resisting Mommy's commands but knew she would have more fun if she listened like a good girl. Octavia wasn't quite as shy as Lexi, but her face and ears still burned with embarrassment as she knelt next to Josie's prone form, "Mommy, can I... can I touch you please?"

Josie sighed with pleasure as Piper's lips met her inner thighs, and it took a heartbeat before she could answer, "You may do what you want Octavia, as long as you do not disturb Daddy until he calls for you."

Octavia gave a squeal of happiness and quickly ran around to join Piper, her hands running up Josie's bare thighs to touch her core, "Is this okay, Mommy?"

"You're both doing very well, my darlings." Piper giggled as Josie opened her legs wider to give both girls better access. Josie let out a moan as Octavia's fingers touched her core, causing goosebumps to erupt across her skin.

"What do we say when we've broken the rules, Lexi?" Liam prompted, massaging her red cheeks.

"I'm sorry, Daddy."

"And?"

Lexi pushed back against his hands, "But, Daddy-"

Whack. Whack.

He gave her two short, sharp smacks, and Lexi squealed, "I'm sorry, Daddy. I won't break the rules again."

"Good girl, Lexi," Liam said as he rubbed her ass again, his cock twitching as he watched the moisture spread and glisten in the light. Liam pulled on the lead, and Lexi came around to face him, still on all fours.

"Open."

Lexi obeyed, opening her mouth wide, her eyes dark with need but eager to please.

Liam pushed his cock into her mouth just as another couple entered the room to watch. He knotted his hand in her hair and tightened the lead with the other, "Keep your throat open, little one, and breathe through your nose."

Whenever Lexi gagged, Liam would pull back a little and whisper to her reassuringly, his cock growing harder as he listened to his wife's moans of pleasure. Precum leaked from his tip, and he pulled away from Lexi. His heart was hammering fiercely, and it took all of his willpower not to cum on her face.

"Did I do something wrong, Daddy?" Lexi asked, her voice soft and uncertain.

"No, little girl, you are doing very well." Liam knelt down next to her and kissed her cheek, "Promise that you will try your very best to be a good girl?"

"I promise, Daddy."

Liam helped her to her feet and scooped her up. Lexi's small frame made it incredibly easy for him to carry her around. He nodded to Carlisle, and the three of them left the room. Liam settled onto one of the couches in the curtained room with Lexi on his lap as Carlisle closed the curtain to afford them a little privacy.

"You were such a good girl, Lexi. I'm very proud of you."

Lexi tucked her head beneath his chin and listened to his heartbeat, "Thank you, Daddy."

Chapter 2

Liam and Josie had hosted their share of play parties, but if they were truly honest with themselves, they preferred to attend rather than host. While hosting had the benefit of setting the mood and providing indirect care for everyone involved, they preferred to be in the thick of things. Not on the sidelines.

Liam and Josie had taken a shower together.

Instead of arriving late as they had thought, Liam and Josie were one of the first of the guests at the party this time. It was a new group of people and happened to be facilitated by a different couple. They had attended nearly every party each of their friends had arranged. Some more strict than others, but overall the couple had never had a bad experience.

"Before we begin," Carlisle spoke up once all the people were accounted for. While Chelsey and Brandon's party was informal and reserved for a small handful of close friends and a lucky select few, Carlisle loved bringing new people into the fold, which meant that there were always formal introductions. He held a clipboard in front of him, from which he was going to be reading the rules, Liam knew. Not because he didn't know them, because everyone who frequented Carlisle's parties knew the rules by heart but because it gave off an official and serious air.

"The rules."

The people in attendance stood quietly and listened intently. A few hands went up to ask a question or to request clarification, and when Carlisle had run through the list, everyone consented to the rules.

"Now, as you can see, this room is pretty drab." Carlisle's comment elicited a few chuckles and elicited a scoff and a playful punch from his husband. It was a standard kitchen, designed in such a way that there was enough room for everyone to sit or stand comfortably. There was a sofa and a few bean bags for seating along with a few chairs around a fairly large coffee table upon which a canteen stood ready to dispense coffee. As usual, there was not a drop of alcohol to be seen.

"This will be our neutral space for the evening. There will be no petting, no touching, no requests. You can come here to talk and wind down, but you will keep it strictly clean."

"If you are uncomfortable about anything at all, come find David or me," Carlisle indicated his husband by his side and added, "If you have a question, ask someone. We are always more than happy to guide you in the right direction."

There were murmurs of agreement. "Follow me," Carlisle said as he swaggered through the kitchen door to his left.

Liam and Josie were hanging back to allow the group to pass first. That's when he saw her. Liam tugged on his wife's elbow and indicated to the short woman in front of them. Her dark hair was carefully braided down her back with what looked like a million tiny butterflies woven in.

After a short tour of the rooms and another emphasis on consent and discussion, Carlisle led them to a large open-plan lounge that was wall-to-wall covered with shag carpeting. There were beanbags, pillows, and blankets everywhere. The lighting was dim and warm, creating a mood of instant comfort and homeliness.

"Kindly find a seat."

People whispered excitedly and plopped down wherever they were, eager to enjoy the planned festivities.

"There are a few new faces in the crowd and more than a few old friends." He grinned devilishly and added, "Let's get the awkward get-to-know-you drivel out of the way. I want each of you to stand and introduce yourself to the group, new and old."

It was pretty standard fare for Liam and Josie who stood up together to indicate that they are a pair - a sort of package deal - and introduced themselves. They were seen to be the resident "Mommy and Daddy" of the group and enjoyed the moniker. While not everyone in attendance followed the same line of enjoyment, there was not a single judgmental face in the crowd.

People stood up at random as they felt the courage to do so, and when the young woman with the glittery butterflies in her braided hair stood up, Liam and Josie paid close attention.

She was dressed in a dark purple onesie underneath denim dungarees, "I'm Cammie." She nervously played with the end of her braid behind her back and licked her lips frequently.

"I'm 29, and I came here tonight to-" her voice shook, and her body was tense, "to make new friends and just be my little ol' self." Her face was beet red when she sat down but the group cheered. Cammie hated the way her cheeks burned when she drew attention to herself.

Soon enough, everyone had been introduced. The group talked animatedly with each other, some turning around in their seats to look behind them, or leaning over others to greet.

"I want you to break up into small groups

now."

What followed was a bonding experience and an exercise in voicing their choice to say 'no.' Carlisle guided them through how to say no, and especially how to remain firm if someone pressed the issue. He also covered and made the groups practice how to deal with another person's 'no.'

Liam had never really had trouble accepting no for an answer. He had learned early on that some people simply weren't interested, and he had learned to deal. Liam found their group's way of coping with being quite interesting. What struck him the most was the more simple of internal responses: "*I* am not what is being rejected, but my offer is."

Liam listened to each of Carlisle's hypothetical offers and descriptions of possible events with a slight amount of amusement. He had each of them reject the request. It ranged anywhere from "Can I touch your hands?" to "Can I watch while three of my friends fill your holes with their cocks."

It broke the ice, and everyone had a laugh. It

emphasized that no matter what, a no is still a no.

When the games were over, Carlisle gave them all a suggestive wink, "Have fun."

Those who wanted to stay and cuddle did so. Other individuals and couples decided to move to rooms more suited to their needs and desires.

One couple was whispering to one another, touching each other's faces and hands. They seemed to delight in doing nothing more than simply being somewhere comfortable with each other.

Cammie was tightly gripping the hand of another Little, who was animatedly talking to her Daddy. Liam recognized Ella, but it was the first time he had seen her attend a party with someone. Liam assumed it was simply because she enjoyed being in her little space by herself rather than accompanied by someone, but that was only a guess. Cammie looked a little nervous but after a whisper from her friend, a smile broke and she eagerly followed behind Ella as she led her to the corner. The pair started piling up pillows and blankets to create a sort of pillow fort around the small table in their corner.

Liam and Josie watched as a few other girls took up another corner of the room and pulled coloring books from their bags. One girl pointed to a pack of crayons, "Can I borrow a crayon from you?"

There was a short moment of hesitation, but the girl consented and passed her the pack. The rest of the exchanges were familiar to Liam. He felt Josie's hand squeeze his. They were both watching the girls as they went about their play. They were laughing and showing off their onesies, stuffies, and one girl even shared her sippy cup with another. The scene was heartwarming, and he felt a surge of protectiveness rush through him. Josie squeezed his hand again and he knew she felt the same.

Hunter, the man that was with Ella and Cammie, looked uncomfortably folded up as he was squeezed into the small space next to Ella. He whispered something to her, and she giggled so hard she fell over. Her display made Cammie grin, and Liam noticed her shoulders relax a little. With a grunt and a flourish, Hunter wriggled out from the tiny space before he was set upon by Ella, who tickled him. He retaliated and ticked back, causing tears to roll down her cheeks from laughter.

"Be good, Ella. I'll be right back."

"Yes, Daddy!" Her eyes followed Hunter to where Liam and Josie were standing, arms wrapped around each other as they watched the display. Ella waved her greeting and returned to her pages, scooting closer to Cammie so that they could share.

He shook hands with both Liam and Josie, who commented on how natural he and Ella looked together.

His laugh was deep but bubbly, "I would hope so, she's my fiancé."

The surprise was evident. "Have you thought about collaring?" The words were out before Josie could stop herself, and Liam suppressed a smile.

Hunter laughed again, "Ella is perfectly capable of expressing her wants and needs. There's no need for a collar to keep unwanted attention away."

"What about Cammie? Is she yours, too?"

"Oh no, not at all. She's a close friend and decided to come with us instead of staying home." Liam and Josie shared a meaningful glance that Hunter found amusing.

"Could you introduce us, you know, formally?" Josie asked a little too eagerly, and Liam squeezed her hand to help temper her excitement. He didn't want her to get her hopes up. There was no guarantee that Cammie would even accept the offer from them.

"She's captivating, isn't she?" Hunter looked over at Cammie, "She has that effect on people, and once they get to know her, *bam,* she's wormed her way into their hearts." He turned back to look at Liam and Josie, a knowing smile on his face.

"Have you ever had your own Little?"

"We have yet to find the perfect match," Liam admitted.

Without a word, Hunter returned to the table. He squatted down next to Ella and spoke softly to the two of them. Liam and Josie could hear nothing over the joyous laughter that came from the other table. The girls were now climbing over each other, tickling and blowing raspberries on any piece of exposed skin they could find. They had made a little game of trying to see who could elicit the most giggles.

There was a tense moment where Liam could feel his heart compress in his chest when Cammie looked at them. She looked so sweet and innocent, and it awoke a primal part of him that just wanted to hold her close and protect her from the world. He knew Josie felt the same way. It was part of why he loved her so much.

Cammie had agreed.

They felt as though their hearts would burst.

The group beckoned them over.

Cammie scooted up to make room for Josie, and Ella sat in Hunter's lap to allow a little room for Liam, who also seemed to be struggling to fit his tall frame into the small space.

"Can I see what you were drawing,

Cammie?" Josie asked. The girl shook her head so vigorously that Josie feared butterflies were going to fly away.

"It's not ready yet," Cammie replied in a small voice.

"That's okay. Then can I draw something for you?" A smile broke open on her face.

Liam hadn't noticed that Hunter and Ella had quietly disappeared until he moved to make himself a bit more comfortable.

"Can you draw a mouse?"

"A mouse?" Liam asked, leaning closer, "Why a mouse?"

"I like them. They're my favorite. So cute and small, and they have big ears!" Cammie's excitement grew as she talked. She told them of the pet mouse she had once had. She tried to draw it for them, too, but couldn't quite succeed. Liam and Josie saw her frustration.

"That's a pretty good mouse, Cammie." Liam offered. He handed her his picture that was also of a mouse, but all they could make out was the big ears and a long tail.

It elicited a small giggle from both Josie and Cammie, but she still looked forlorn.

"I can teach you how to draw a mouse," Josie said as she slowly reached her hand across the table to Cammie. She let it rest there - an invitation.

Cammie wasn't sure what to think of Liam, or Josie, for that matter. They seemed kind enough, but again, so did her previous Daddy. It wasn't something she wanted to discuss - not here, not now.

But how could she explain to them that their kindness was actually hurting her?

Cammie abruptly got up, dropped the crayon she was holding, whispered a soft, "No, thank you." followed by an apology, and disappeared.

***

Cammie entered the kitchen, feeling a little lost, a little unsure of herself. While she hadn't had many expectations, she did hope to hit it off with *someone*. She felt stressed and was on the verge of tears.

"What do you need, honey?" David was at her side in an instant. He seemed to have an instinct for when people felt...out of their depth.

"Just a cup of coffee." Cammie's reply was curt, she realized, and added, "Pretty please. I'm dying for a fix."

David smiled, content with her request. Politeness was key.

"Do you have cream? Or whipped cream? I'll even take half-and-half if you have it." Cammie asked as she looked over the contents of the little fridge they were permitted to use. She stopped herself from asking for alcohol. It was a rule. No alcohol anywhere on the property, but she felt as though she needed it.

She had met a lovely couple: Liam and Josie. But to her, they seemed uninterested. They had talked and played and drawn pictures, but she wanted more. She wanted to cuddle but wasn't sure how to ask for it. She wanted them to take care of her. Liam and Josie. So she turned to the next best thing: whipped cream.

David set the can next to her, where she was seated at the table, scooping a ton of sugar into her mug, "Want to talk about it?"

Cammie looked startled, and her face turned beet red again.

"Not a lot of people want whipped cream with their coffee. With other things, yes, but not with coffee. Especially not in these circles." David's eyes glittered, and a smile tugged at his lips, and his gaze softened, "I know an emotional soother when I see one, honey."

At that, he squirted a generous amount into her coffee and pulled a small shaker from the cupboard, "My secret stash."

"Chocolate sprinkles!" Cammie generously covered the cream in sprinkles and immediately dug in.

A soft chuckle came from the doorway. Josie hadn't meant to eavesdrop but was delighted to see

Cammie so excited over something she thought mundane. Given her abrupt departure from their table, Josie was glad to see her smile at all.

"No, no, don't stop on my account," Josie said as Cammie made to put the cup down. She suppressed another chuckle at Cammie's white mustache and poured herself a cup of coffee. Josie sat down across of Cammie. Close enough to feed her desire to take care of the woman but also far enough away as to not suffocate her.

"Listen," Josie said after an awkward moment of silence, "if we came on too strong, I'm sorry."

After another pause, Cammie broke the silence, "It's not that, Josie. I guess my expectations were a little skewed."

"What do you mean?"

"I-" Cammie paused, and a shadow passed over her features. She *really* needed a drink right now. "My life is a mess. I expected to find some way to escape that tonight. If anything, I think all I did was make an even bigger mess." Cammie scooped some cream with her finger and stuck it in her mouth. She could tell Josie was waiting for her to finish. Most people would blunder on and change the focus to themselves. Cammie appreciated it, then, with a deep sigh, added, "I actually don't know what I was looking for."

Josie looked at the girl in front of her. They weren't that far apart in age, but Cammie really did give off this vulnerability that made Josie ache to hold her and promise her everything will be okay.

"That's the thing about messes, Cammie. You can always clean them up with the right help." Josie smiled reassuringly and handed Cammie a napkin for her whipped cream mustache, "Come find me if you want to talk."

Josie disappeared through the doorway, and Cammie poked the cream with the tip of her finger and licked it off.

David was busying himself at the oven, pulling a fresh batch of cookies from its depths.

"David?" Cammie asked, "How well do you know Liam and Josie?"

"Honey, they are the fiercest, kindest, and most generous people I have ever had the pleasure to meet." David handed her a warm cookie and bit into one himself.

"But-" he said, between bites, "-you should spend time with them to see for yourself. Different strokes." David savored another cookie and returned to the oven to bake the next batch. "It's okay if you don't hit it off with anyone. Don't feel pressured to have this be that moment for you. Sometimes it takes a couple of tries. Life's funny like that."

"Thank you for the coffee, David," Cammie said, and her heartfelt a little lighter as she took a bite of her cookie.

***

The one-on-one diaper playroom was fully stocked along with a side table filled with lotions, creams, and powders. A single bed was pushed up against the wall, right next to the changing table.

There was a second, larger bed opposite the first, that could accommodate snuggles, cuddles, and possibly other forms of play if there was consent. Liam and Josie knew that there would be nothing more than caregiving today. It was what the three of them had agreed to. Cammie didn't want anything more, and truth be told, neither did Josie or Liam.

It was not a private room by any means, but it did preclude anyone from joining unless they had permission from all parties present.

Cammie stood just inside the doorway, a red blush creeping up her neck again. Josie noticed, "What's the matter, little one?"

Her voice was so low that Josie had to put her ear right up to Cammie's lips to hear, "I had an accident." Cammie's voice was breaking.

Josie held her close and hushed her.

"There's nothing to be ashamed about, little mouse." Liam's soothing voice caused her to look up at him with wide, trusting eyes, tears brimming them.

"Let's get you cleaned up. Then we can do something together."

"Can we read a story?"

"Whatever you want, little one," Josie said, kissing Cammie's flushed cheek as she guided her to the changing station. Cammie's face lit up, momentarily forgetting her wet diaper.

Cammie unclipped the dungaree straps with a little difficulty, but she had insisted on doing that herself, and she let the overalls crumple to a heap at her feet. Liam had laid out a soft, clean sheet over the bed.

"Good job, little one." Josie helped Cammie get up on the single bed and instructed her to lie on her back. Josie carefully spread her legs apart and reached between them to unclip the onesie. Liam had started pulling out cream and baby powder and setting them on the end table within Josie's reach.

She pushed the hem of the onesie over Cammie's soft, warm skin, delighting in the goosebumps that were spreading from her touch. The diaper crinkled as Cammie squirmed and giggled, "That tickles, Mommy."

Josie chuckled, her smile was contagious, "Hold still, please."

Cammie stuck her thumb in her mouth and watched both Liam and Josie as the first fastening was removed with a rough tearing noise, then the other. Josie carefully pulled the front of the diaper down. Her breath caught in her throat. Cammie's pussy lips were shaved clean. There was not a hair or blemish in sight, except for one, tiny beauty mark.

Getting her voice back, Josie instructed Cammie to lift her hips so that they could remove the diaper completely. Cammie did as she was told, dutifully lifting her hips, providing Josie with a delicious view.

"Look at that! Not such a big mess, little girl. You're doing well." Josie exclaimed and handed the wet diaper off to Liam, who carefully folded it closed and discarded it into the bin.

Josie grabbed a wet wipe and started to clean

Cammie off. She started with the inner thigh where some urine had been smeared. Josie moved the wipe in circles, first the one leg, then the other. Cammie spread her legs, her face flushed with something other than shame this time. "Don't forget the most important part, Mommy."

Liam's cock jerked. Her gesture wasn't as innocent as the rest of their play, but he stilled the urge to touch her.

Josie used a clean wipe and started on her lips. The cloth was so thin that it may as well not have been there. Her fingers ran over the swollen nub, and Cammie moaned softly. Her own core burned in response. Josie continued cleaning her baby girl up, making sure to wipe down every spot.

Liam handed Josie the bottle of baby cream.

"What's that for, Mommy?" Cammie asked.

"It's cream so that the diaper doesn't give your soft bottom a rash," Josie said.

Josie massaged the cream into Cammie's soft ass and over her mound, careful not to let her fingers linger too long.

Liam handed her a fresh diaper. Again, Cammie lifted her hips. Josie set the diaper in place, and Cammie dropped her hips, her thumb still in her mouth and her big eyes watching them.

Josie sprinkled some baby powder into the palms of her hands and ran them over her skin. The scent was fresh and lovely. It reminded her of home. Cammie felt at ease. They were polite and followed her wishes, even if her little body had betrayed her when Josie touched her.

The diaper was fastened, and she was told to get up. Carefully, the fabric of the onesie was rolled down and refastened.

"Do you want to put your dungarees back on?"

Cammie shook her head.

"Use your words, little mouse," Liam said.

"No, Mommy."

"Then, I think you should hang it up over the chair so that it doesn't wrinkle." Josie helped Cammie shake it out and fold it carefully over the armrest of the only chair in the room.

"Good job, Cammie."

Liam got comfortable on the bed and patted the spot next to him. Cammie looked expectantly at Josie, who nodded and patted her bottom, "You go snuggle, and I'll pick out a book for us to read." Cammie squealed with joy and launched herself into Liam's arms. A tickle war ensued, and Liam's rich laughter mixed in with Cammie's sweet voice made Josie's heart swell. This is what she wanted, and it was amazing.

"Alright you two, what do you want to read?" Josie asked and made herself comfortable on Cammie's other side as her fits of laughter slowly quieted.

"What are our choices?" Liam asked, reaching out to tuck a strand of Josie's hair. He felt at home.

"Well, there is Little Red Riding Hood," Josie suggested, "Daddy can make all the noises for the Big Bad Wolf. He's amazing."

"Oh, no, that sounds too scary!" Cammie commented and pulled her stockinged legs up.

Liam wrapped his arms around her and kissed the top of her head, "It's okay, little mouse, it's just a story."

"Or how about a story just for you?" Josie ventured, "The Tales of Despereaux. It's about a little mouse who acts too different from other mice, so they try to teach him to stop being different."

"Were they mean to him, Mommy?"
Josie smiled, "Let's find out together."
They sat snuggled together on the bed, Cammie listening intently. She gasped in the right places, laughed when the little mouse did something funny and was scared when he was in danger. Liam had made the voices for the bad guys, deepening it to almost a growl. He made his voice light and squeaky for the little mouse. He also made the noises of the pots bubbling in the kitchen, or the sound of a mouse chewing on paper.
Cammie was enthralled. Liam and Josie were caring and kind. They let her ask questions. They

held her. And they played with her. They
demanded nothing.

Chapter 3

On a rare weekend off together, Liam and Josie lay in each other's arms, the curtains drawn against the mid-morning sunlight.

"I have a surprise for you," Liam whispered as he kissed her neck and collarbone, eliciting a sigh of content from Josie.

"But that means we have to get up," he said as he immediately rolled out of bed, and Josie protested.

"I was comfortable." Josie huffed and sat up, hair mussed, and her lips swollen. Liam pulled in to kiss her, "It'll be fun, I promise."

***

Liam's first stop, and to Josie's surprise, was a little lingerie shop.

"I'm here to collect my order," Liam said,

his arms still around his wife, holding her close to him. The staff looked on in envy. Josie could tell by the way their eyes glossed over that they were imagining Liam doing all kinds of things to them.

A faint blush crept onto her cheek when she noticed a few of those salacious looks were aimed at her. The attention had started a warm tingle in the center of her body that steadily grew warmer and started to pulse as Liam unperturbed ran his hand down her body.

"Mr. Everhart, your order." The saleswoman carefully placed the package in front of him and unfolded the tissue paper that was wrapped around it. Liam stepped close, removed the garment from the parcel, and held it up for Josie to inspect.

A black, snakeskin patterned lace outfit with leather ties, garter straps, and an adjustable choker. When Josie stroked the fabric, it was much softer than it appeared. Smooth and almost as soft as silk.

"It's gorgeous, Liam." Josie breathed.

"Would the lady like to be fitted for the garment?" The question seemed innocent enough, but neither Josie nor Liam missed the lustful undertone at the suggestion of the saleswoman.

A twinkle in her eye told Liam that Josie was more than willing.

Liam waited outside the dressing room as Josie changed into her gift. Josie stripped naked and looked at her sleek, defined form in the mirror. As she slid into the garment, the soft lace and cool leather contrasted one another, caressing her skin and causing goosebumps to spread across her body.

Josie admired her reflection. Liam knew exactly what she wanted. The corset hugged her body, accentuating her curves. The adjustable leather straps that ran between her breasts were tantalizing. Josie pulled on the stockings that came with the garment and clipped them to the garter straps. It fit like a glove.

Josie emerged from the dressing room with a flourish, grinning broadly at the breathless expressions on the faces of her audience.

Cammie, tucked into the corner and trying to keep her head down, turned to look at the commotion. Her heart jumped into her throat, and she blinked a couple of times to make sure that she wasn't hallucinating.

"Josie," she whispered, and an immediate heat flooded through her. There was no denying that the woman was built like a goddess. Cammie's feet guided her, unbidden, closer...closer...close enough that she could almost reach out and touch Josie.

Their eyes met, and a spark ignited deep inside of her. The garment only alluded to the forbidden places on the woman's body, but Cammie's desire built regardless. She shuffled, becoming a little uncomfortable but kept her eyes locked on Josie's.

Cammie was still holding her bralette and panties, she realized, as Josie closed the gap between them. Liam also only noticed Cammie now, and a warm smile crinkled his eyes, "Cammie, what a pleasant surprise."

Her return greeting was a little half-hearted, but Liam knew the reason behind it. Josie's walk was dominating, her hips swaying seductively. Josie's gaze drifted to the garments Cammie was clutching, and a blush crept up her neck. It was a simple style, but still cute. Pink ribbons adorned the straps of the bralette and the front of the panties.

***

"Here," Josie said and handed a stack of clothes to Cammie. Instinctively, Cammie took them but stuttered out an apology, "J-Josie, I appreciate you helping me choose something, but I really can't afford any of this."

Not a complete lie. Cammie had *some* funds in her account but had been planning on spending the evening at a bar. Something to take her mind off of her job, her life, and her unsatisfied sex life. Hopefully, getting buzzed just enough that she wouldn't mind going home with a complete stranger.

When Cammie hesitated, Josie placed a gentle hand on hers, "You don't have to get anything you want to, Cammie. It's for completely selfish reasons," Josie said. "I want to see what they would look like on you."

Cammie smiled, a little turned on at the thought of Josie seeing her completely naked. With a small nod, Cammie agreed and headed to the changing room, Josie, in tow.

***

Cammie had really started to relax around Liam and Josie. She watched how the two interacted with each other and with others. She had taken David's advice and had taken the chance to get to know them.

They both intimidated her, but she doubted it was purposeful. Whenever Josie noticed that Cammie was feeling uncomfortable, she had gone out of her way to set Cammie at ease. Josie had joked about the pink bralette and panties, but it was lighthearted and fun. After seeing how confident Josie was and how unsuggestive any of her comments or questions were, Cammie had felt silly for being ashamed about buying such spicy undergarments.

As the day wore on, the pair had invited Cammie along to lunch, and eventually, they made their way to a nearby park where they could enjoy the rest of the beautiful day.

Just as Josie had made Cammie feel at ease, Liam had done the same. Liam would subtly change topics or phrase questions in such a way that Cammie didn't feel forced to answer, but rather that she had *wanted* to answer them. Liam had asked her about her job. Her parents, her friends, and soon enough, the sun was starting to set.

"How long have the two of you..." Cammie trailed off.

"Been Caregivers?" Liam said, finishing Cammie's question.

"Yes," Cammie replied, looking down at her

feet.

There was a small pause before Liam answered, "A year or so into our marriage, we started talking about fantasies. We met some people, made some friends, and went to our first play party."

"That was about five years ago," Josie added.

"How many Littles do you take care of?"

"We stand in as we need to, but we have never officially adopted a Little of our own."

"Would you want to?" Cammie asked, but hastily added, "I mean, the other Littles seem to flock around the two of you, and you seem happy. I just mean-"

Josie laughed, "We understand what you mean, Cammie."

"We *are* happy, little mouse. We have grown to love them, even if they have their own full-time Daddies or Mommies," Liam said.

"We want to, but it's not always possible," Josie added.

"Would you-" Cammie pursed her lips, her

heart was hammering in her chest so hard she was sure than Liam and Josie could hear it, "would you want me?"

The split second of time that followed the request was the longest of her life, but Cammie kept a brave face and braced for the worst.

"Cammie, sweetheart, we would love nothing more," Liam whispered.

Liam and Josie felt as though they had struck gold. This sweet, shy girl wanted them. Both of them, as they were.

Tears were threatening to fall, and Cammie looked away. It was tenuous, but hope bloomed in her chest as she whispered, "Promise? You're not just making fun of me?"

"We would never make fun of you, Cammie," Josie said, holding her hand out to Cammie. She scooted closer and hugged Josie, listening to her heartbeat and feeling the warmth of her body through the dress.

"It's getting late," Josie said.

"Cammie, would you like to come home

with us?" Liam asked.

Cammie pulled away from Josie to stare at them. Liam was smiling reassuringly. "It would be no imposition, Cammie," he added.

"We would like to have your company if you'd do us the honor," Josie said, patting her hand.

Josie's next words weren't quite as innocent. This time Cammie knew the question held more than the prospect of simply visiting them for dinner. Perhaps it was the way it was phrased, or by the way, Josie's gaze darkened as she looked at her, but Cammie could see her attraction clear as day. "You can stay over if you'd like."

***

Cammie was in awe. The house was the most beautiful place she had ever seen. It was breathtaking. Magnificent. Cammie ran out of words to use to describe it. It wasn't enormous, but it was imposing in its sleek architecture.

"The house has been in my family for years," Liam said. The stunned look on Cammie's face filled him with pride. "You two go inside while I grab our things."

Cammie followed behind Josie as she let herself in. The house was more beautiful inside than it was out, and Cammie gawked.

"Come now, little one, let's show you around." Josie hooked her arm through Cammie's, and off they went. By the time they had worked their way through the house, both upstairs and the cozy little yard outside, Liam had brought in all their shopping bags and had poured them each something to drink, making himself comfortable on the leather couch in the living room.

"I have something I think you would like, little one," Josie said as Cammie made herself comfortable next to Liam on the couch.

Curiosity got the better of her, and Cammie hopped to her feet. Josie handed Cammie a small gift-wrapped package, "I saw how much you liked." Cammie tore it open, her eyes watering a little, "I can keep it?"

"Yes, little one. It's all yours." Josie said. Cammie jumped excitedly and hugged her gift to her chest. It was the pink dress that she had fallen in love with at the store. It was covered in yellow bows and frills of white and gray. She threw her arms around Josie, pressing herself against her body, saying 'thank you' over and over again.

The longer she was pressed against Josie, the more aware she became of her body. What Cammie had seen in the store was now highlighted and enhanced by touch. Cammie could feel the heat of her skin against hers; she could smell Josie's scent. Cammie felt the urge to kiss her. And then she did. It was just a light peck. To say, thank you. But then Cammie kissed her again, and this time she let her lips linger. Cammie savored the feel of feminine lips against hers, so soft and demanding at the same time. Josie's arms tightened, and she kissed Cammie back, losing herself in that single moment. Josie's tongue searched out hers. Cammie broke the kiss by stepping back, her face flushed, and her breathing a little uneven.

"Can I go try it on, Mommy?" Cammie asked.

"Of course you can, Cammie," Josie said and licked her lips, "but show Daddy the dress after you've put it on. He hasn't seen it yet."

Cammie dashed into the nearest room and changed, stripping her tight jeans and crop top off. She had stripped completely naked, enjoying the freedom. She pulled the dress over her head and smiled as she ran her fingertips over the little gray mouse embroidered over her heart. Cammie's lips still tingled where they had touched Josie's, and she let her hand roam, touching herself.

The excitement of what was to come was slowly building up within her, and Cammie stroked herself, loving the sensation.

Cammie ran back to where Liam and Josie were sitting in the lounge and interrupted their talk with her outburst, "Look how pretty my new dress is, Daddy!"

Cammie threw herself onto the couch and locked

her arms around them, nuzzling their faces excitedly.

"Little mouse," Liam's voice was firm, and his look sucked away just a little of the excitement as he carefully pulled her away from him.

"Yes, Daddy?" Cammie asked, embarrassment flooding her.

"Good little girls don't interrupt people when they're talking, do they?"

"No, Daddy."

"Are you a good girl, Cammie?"

"Yes, Daddy. I'm sorry, Daddy. I just got all excited."

Liam chuckled and stroked her arm to let her know he wasn't angry, "Good, now what is it you wanted to show us?"

Cammie got up off of the couch and twirled; the little ribbons and frills dancing as she moved. "See, I look almost like a princess," Cammie whispered gleefully as she twirled again.

"Oh, but you *are* a princess, Cammie." Josie beamed.

"Only a real princess could look as beautiful as you," Liam cooed and motioned for Cammie to come a little closer.

"Can I sit on your lap, Daddy?" Cammie asked, holding the folds of her dress in her fists and swishing the skirt around playfully.

"Yes, little mouse."

Cammie carefully sat herself down in Liam's lap. She could feel his hardness pressed against her thigh, and it caused a jolt of pleasure to shoot through her.

"Am I hurting you, Daddy?"

"Not at all, sweetheart." Liam's voice was thick. Not a lie, but his cock was straining against the zipper of his jeans, which was beginning to sit uncomfortably.

Cammie wrapped her arms around Liam's neck and pressed her face into his shoulder. She felt comfortable, warm, and perfectly safe.

Cammie, feeling a little naughty, pulled away from Liam, looked him dead in the eye, and licked his cheek. Taking advantage of the brief moment of surprise, Cammie disengaged and darted away, giggling hysterically.

Josie laughed and watched as Liam set off after her. The laughter echoing in the house was a beautiful sound.

"Be careful you two," She called, still smiling broadly. Cammie whipped past her, her skirt lifting up high behind her as she jumped over the furniture. After a few more minutes, Liam and Cammie fell to the carpet at Josie's feet out of breath.

"Join us, Mommy!"

Liam held his hand out to her, and Josie slid onto the floor. Their lips met, and fire burned between them.

Liam felt Cammie fiddle with the buckle on his belt. She was biting her bottom lip and rubbing his cock through the fabric of his jeans.

"Mommy, can you help me, please?"

Josie showed Cammie how to undo Liam's belt with one hand, and the girl beamed, "I did it!"

"You're a smart girl, little mouse," Liam

whispered, his voice husky and deep.

Josie instructed Cammie how to undo the buttons on the jeans, and together, they freed his throbbing cock. Cammie immediately wrapped her warm hands around it and began squeezing softly. He grabbed a handful of hair and guided Cammie's lips to the head of his cock.

Josie got on her knees and demonstrated, "Carefully, like this."

Cammie watched as Josie's expert hands stroked Liam's cock, and her tongue flicked over the head, causing his cock to twitch uncontrollably.

"Slow," he commanded.

Josie grinned broadly at Cammie, a naughty twinkle in her eye, "You try, baby girl."

Cammie felt moisture pool between her legs. She had decided to go commando under the dress and felt daring for doing so. Her heart raced, exhilarated. Cammie copied Josie's movements almost exactly, first stroking him with her hands, then flicking her tongue over and around the head of his swollen member. It twitched, and a bead of liquid formed at the tip.

Then, locking eyes with Liam, she opened her mouth and sucked the head of his cock into it, flicking her tongue over the sensitive tip.

"Good girl," Josie said as she ran her hands over Cammie's thighs, feeling her quake. Her own body was screaming for release, but she wanted to make sure Cammie knew how to please her Daddy properly.

"Slowly, and be careful not to hurt Daddy with your teeth, little girl."

Cammie continued stroking Liam's thick cock with her hands and mouth, enjoying the taste of him. She suckled on the head of his cock and delighted it the blissed-out look on Liam's face.

Josie gently pulled Cammie away and pressed her lips to Cammie's. She tasted faintly of Liam and sugar. Josie kissed her harder, running her hand down Cammie's small body, tasting her with her tongue.

Josie broke off the kiss and tucked a strand of hair behind Cammie's ear.

"Watch me carefully, little one."

She showed Cammie how to take all of Liam's thick cock into her mouth and into her throat. Cammie watched as Liam's eyes' rolled to the back of his head just as Josie's tongue caressed the underside of his balls. Josie continued sucking Liam's cock, pulling away until just his tip remained in her mouth, then expertly swallowing his cock until the whole thing was no longer visible to Cammie. Liam groaned his pleasure.

"Can I try, Mommy?" Cammie asked, edging closer, feeling moisture coat her inner thighs.

"Not yet, little mouse," Liam said and sat up as Josie finally released him. His cock jerked wildly as he suppressed the urge to cum.

"Why not, Daddy?" Cammie asked, not bothering to hide the hurt, "Did I do something wrong?"

"You did wonderfully, Cammie," Liam said thickly, "but I want you to help Mommy undress while I catch my breath."

Cammie's eyes glittered as she understood, and

Josie helped her to her feet. Josie turned around and pulled her hair out of the way to give Cammie access to the zipper of her dress. Cammie, driven by the super-charged sexual tension between them, unzipped the dress slowly, making sure to let her fingers caress her skin as they trailed down her back. Electricity passed between them.

Josie stepped out of the dress and stood to face Cammie and Liam. Her undergarments were simple, not at all like the gift Liam had gotten her earlier that day. Her hands caressed Josie's breasts, testing their weight, and her fingers slipped under the wired support, stroking the bare skin of her breasts. Cammie's fingers found the front clasp.

Cammie licked her lips.

"Keep going, little mouse, you're doing so well." Her body throbbed with need at Liam's words; his cock still out and rock hard, precum glistening on the head. Cammie gently grabbed the elastic of Josie's thong and slid her hands down her outer thighs. Cammie's face was now perfectly aligned with Josie's swollen lips, and she could see moisture glistening between their folds. Josie's scent was intoxicating, and without asking, Cammie leaned forward and flicked her tongue over Josie's slit, tasting the dew that glittered there.

"Stop," Josie said.

"Why?" Cammie couldn't suppress her whine of frustration and sat back on her heels, looking up at Josie with a mix of irritation and desperation. She wanted to taste all of Josie, and she wanted to feel Liam's cock pushing inside of her. Cammie wanted both of them to hold her while she pleasured them and they pleasured her.

"Girls who don't listen to their Mommies get punished." Liam's voice sent another jolt of heat through her as he wrapped his arms around Josie from behind and slid his fingers into her wet pussy, letting it coat his fingers.

"It's not fair, Daddy!"

"Cammie." A warning clear in Liam's voice.

"But Daddy."

"Stand up, little mouse," Liam commanded, still playing with his wife's pussy.

Cammie stood, pouting. It was a bad move, and she knew it, but Cammie wasn't going to be denied.

"Go to the room and wait for me." Liam's voice held the promise of a good spanking, and Cammie could already feel her bottom sting. Cammie folded her arms and huffed.

"Don't make Daddy repeat himself, Cammie." Josie's voice imitated Liam's in its seriousness.

"No." Her words were barely cold when Liam pulled his belt free from his jeans. Cammie gulped and involuntarily took a step back.

"Bend over, now."

Cammie shivered. She heard the steel in his voice but also felt the sexual tension climb.

"Daddy."

Liam closed the distance between them and gently, and with practiced movement, spun Cammie around, and bent her over the armrest of the couch. He lifted the skirt of the dress over her ass and paused.

"No panties?" Liam asked, unable to hide his surprise. Cammie could feel his cock press against her bare ass cheek, and she swallowed in anticipation.

"No, Daddy."

Liam stroked Cammie's bare ass, the skin was soft, and her cheeks were firm. Liam pulled back a little to allow room for what came next, "Count."

"Daddy, no, I-"

Whack.

Her ass stung, and the sound was ringing in her ears.

"One."

Whack.

"Two."

Cammie squeezed her eyes shut as Liam spanked her with his belt. It wasn't hard enough to leave a mark, but it was hard enough to make his point. When she reached ten, he set the belt down and gently rubbed her now red cheeks. He spread them apart, letting his fingers touch her pussy lips.

Cammie quivered.

"It looks like our little girl enjoyed that, Josie."

Josie took Liam's place behind Cammie. Cammie was trembling and panting, "I'm sorry, Daddy."

Josie's tongue surprised Cammie as she pushed it between her pussy lips, flicking her swollen clit. She gasped and moaned out loud. Josie inserted first one finger, then two into her dripping pussy.

"Are you going to behave now, baby girl?" Josie whispered as she kissed the soft skin of her ass, letting her fingers slide in and out of Cammie's pussy.

"Yes, Mommy." With that, Josie sped up her strokes, and Cammie came hard. Her body twitched, and she screamed out loud, "Fuck!"

Liam thrust his cock into her spasming pussy, and Cammie swore again. He pulled out and, panting, Cammie tried to push back onto his cock, "I'm sorry, Daddy, don't stop."

"What do we say?" Liam used the flat of his hand and spanked her.

"Please, Daddy, please put it back in." Liam pushed in slowly as he rubbed her raw ass cheek. He spanked her again as he pulled out.

"Daddy." Cammie was pleading with him. Her moans grew louder with each firm *whack* and soon orgasmed a second time, her pussy clamping down on his cock, and she writhed beneath him. Josie crawled onto the couch and kissed Cammie, drawing more moans from her. Josie positioned herself and spread her legs, presenting her own swollen and wet pussy to Cammie, "Please lick Mommy's pussy, little girl." Cammie licked her lips and obeyed, her body still twitching, and her mind foggy. Josie threw her head back and moaned, grabbing a fistful of hair, she kept Cammie's lips pressed to her pussy lips, feeling her sweet, warm tongue flick and probe, drawing pleasure from her.

"That's right, little one, just like that." Liam encouraged Cammie. The look of ecstasy on his wife's face and the tight pussy stroking his cock brought him dangerously close to an orgasm. Liam slowed his strokes, and with his thumb, he circled Cammie's ass hole, coating it in her own juices. She moaned as he slowly pushed a finger into her tight hole, her body tensing.

"Relax your muscles, little mouse."
Cammie obeyed, and he started a slow rhythm, matching his thrusts into her pussy.

It was a new and strange sensation, but it heightened her arousal, making her body twitch again, "Oh, Daddy."

Liam grunted and pulled his cock out of Cammie's pussy. After working her ass for a few more minutes, Cammie's moans were nearly as loud as his wife's. Josie had her head thrown back, her fingers pinching and pulling her own nipples as Cammie's fingers worked their way in and out of her wetness.

Liam pressed the head of his thick member against Cammie's lubricated ass hole. Cammie gasped and pushed back slightly.

"Daddy, put your cock in my ass and make me cum again," Cammie cried out as he pushed inside of her. His cock stretching her ass hole, filling her to the brim.

Josie orgasmed loudly, bucking against Cammie's fingers, her face flushed from pleasure. She saw the look of concentration on Liam's face as he attempted to keep himself in check.

"Tell Daddy what you want, Cammie," Josie whispered, running her thumb over Cammie's bottom lip. Josie wanted to see the look on Liam's face as he filled their little girl with his hot cum.

"Fuck me hard, Daddy," Cammie said breathlessly as she waited for him to thrust into her tight hole. Her body had adjusted to his size and relaxed accordingly. Her pussy twitched in anticipation as Liam massaged her ass cheeks, then gripped her hips, holding her in place.

"Please, Daddy?" Cammie begged.

Liam lost control as his baby girl begged for his cock. He spread her ass cheeks apart and started pumping his cock in and out of Cammie's ass. Cammie pushed back onto his cock and moaned loudly. Her voice caused his cock to throb and twitch as he fucked her.

"Make me cum, Daddy." Cammie could feel her body on the edge. It was a different feeling, more intense. Cammie's body exploded as she orgasmed violently. Her eyes rolled to the back of her head as she screamed.

Liam thrust himself deep into Cammie's ass hole. Her orgasm was causing the muscles in her body to clench and tighten around him. Liam came instantly. His cock spurted cum deep into her ass. He threw his head back and clenched his teeth, groaning loudly as his orgasm ripped through him. Spent, Liam pulled his cock free and joined the girls on the floor.

They lay intertwined on the soft plush carpet of the living room, panting. Cammie could feel her body still twitching from her previous orgasms. Her brain was fuzzy, and her limbs weak.

Josie was planting soft kisses over her eyes and face. Every part of her skin was sensitive to touch, and Cammie moaned in response as Josie drew her nails across the skin on Cammie's inner thighs.

Liam wrapped his arms around Cammie and pulled her close to him, burying his nose in her hair. She smelled of a woman, sex, and flowers. His cock jerked, and he pressed it against Cammie's ass, making her moan again.

***

When they finally caught their breath after another round of play, it was well close to midnight.

"Let's get you cleaned up, little girl," Josie whispered as she moved to stand. Her legs were trembling, but her footing was steady. She held her hand out to Cammie, who took it, still dazed.

The girl had a glow about her that Josie knew all too well. Liam was adept at drawing even the most reluctant of orgasms from anyone.

Together the two women made their way to the bathroom. Josie added some bubble bath to the stream and watched as the warm water flowed into the tub, and steam started to fill the air.

Josie helped Cammie into the tub and watched as she sighed and sank further down into the water. She allowed her to sit in silence for as long as she needed. Cammie felt the heaviness of her eyes and yawned, "Mommy, I'm sleepy."

"You need to wash yourself first, little Cammie. Then we can snuggle in bed together, okay?"

"Okay, Mommy." Cammie's movements were sluggish, and she dropped the bottle of body wash with a messy splash. Cammie giggled tiredly, "Please help me, Mommy."

Josie helped her lather and wash every inch of her body.

"I'm done now, Mommy," Cammie said proudly after she rinsed the soap from her skin all by herself.

"Good girl. Time to get out."

Cammie stood carefully and held her arms out. Josie wrapped her in a large, fluffy towel.

"Thank you, Mommy."

Josie guided Cammie to the kitchen and sat her

down in the chair and kissed her forehead, "Daddy will make you a bottle, little one."

"Wait! Where are you going, Mommy?" Cammie asked sleepily, trying to wriggle the chair around in order to see Josie.

"Mommy's going to go take a shower, Cammie," Liam said, drawing her attention back to him. While Cammie had been in the bath, Liam had taken a shower of his own. He smelled fresh and wore soft, silky-looking sweatpants, and Cammie could make out the length of his cock as the material caressed it.

"Okay, Daddy." Cammie was still wrapped in the warm embrace of the towel and was slowly starting to fall asleep in her seat. Liam chuckled, "Come, little mouse, here's your bottle."

Liam handed her a baby bottle that was filled with a creamy looking liquid. The girl hadn't eaten since their early lunch, and he was sure she was famished. It was close to two in the morning, and he could feel his own stomach grumble unhappily. He had mixed up a serving of a good quality meal replacer for her and added an extra bit of vanilla syrup to sweeten it up. Cammie had shown to have a pretty big sweet tooth, both at lunch and during the last play party, they had attended.

"What flavor did you make it, Daddy?" Cammie asked at the same time she popped the nipple in her mouth.

"Vanilla ice cream."

Cammie smiled happily and continued drinking, her eyes drooping a little more, "Daddy, can we go to bed now?"

"Of course we can, little mouse, as soon as we get you dressed." Liam scooped her up easily enough and carried her to the spare bedroom where their toys were kept. Cammie was too sleepy to notice her surroundings, except how soft and inviting the bed felt beneath her.

Cammie sighed happily as she sucked on the bottle, enjoying the creamy vanilla taste. It was thicker than a milkshake and just as sweet.

Liam had brought some of Cammie's things in from the living room. He pulled a diaper from one of the bags and set it down on the end table. Liam gently pulled Cammie into a seated position, and the towel slipped from her shoulders.

"Stand for Daddy, please."

Cammie obeyed and was unsteady on her feet. Liam removed the towel and made her lie down again. Liam gripped Cammie by the ankles and lifted her legs and ass into the air as he swiftly slid the diaper underneath her.

Cammie giggled, "You're strong, Daddy."

Liam fastened the velcro straps of the diaper and turned to another of Cammie's bags. He had spied a onesie in there earlier and looked for it now. When he turned back, Cammie had the strangest look on her face. It took him a second to figure it out, and then Cammie giggled, "Sorry, Daddy."

She had wet herself.

Just then, Josie came into the room, saw the guilt on Cammie's face, the slight annoyance on Liam's, and chuckled, "What did you do, little one?"

"I had an accident," Cammie whispered and her cheeks turning a bright pink. She put the bottle back in her mouth and continued drinking.

Liam shook his head and smiled, "Our baby forgot to use the little girl's room before getting ready for bed."

"I'll grab a clean one," Josie said.

Again, Liam gripped Cammie by the ankles, "Ready?" She nodded, and he hoisted her up, causing the girl to giggle. He pulled the wet diaper free and Josie replaced it with a fresh one. She wiped Cammie down with a couple of baby wipes and then patted her bottom dry with the towel.

"I'm sorry, Daddy, I didn't mean to make a mess," Cammie whispered.

"It's okay, little mouse, accidents happen." Liam gently stroked her hair as Josie continued to fix the diaper.

When she was done, Josie helped Cammie into her new onesie, clipped it closed, and handed her over to Liam. Cammie had finished her bottle by now but was still suckling on the nipple, her eyes closed. Liam lifted Cammie and held her to him, her head resting on his shoulders.

Josie cleaned up and followed behind Liam as the pair made their way to the main bedroom. Liam carefully lay Cammie down on the bed, and she squirmed to get comfortable, still sucking on the empty bottle.

"Here you go, sweetheart," Josie said, and removed the bottle, replacing it with Cammie's brand new paci. Without opening her eyes, Cammie adjusted it and continued suckling, a smile on her face.

Josie smiled at her sleeping form, "Our little girl is wonderful, Liam."

Liam and Josie, tired, but happy, crawled into bed with their little girl. Josie snuggled up to Cammie and wrapped her arms around her. Cammie mumbled something in her sleep and snuggled deeper into Josie's embrace.

Liam had gotten into bed on Cammie's other side and watched as his girls slept. He stroked Cammie's hair, content.

***

Early the next morning, Cammie had snuck out of bed and went to grab a shower before work. Cammie was busy making coffee when Liam and Josie emerged from the room, completely dressed.

"Don't worry about your car," Josie said. "I've already made a call to have it safely transported to where you need it. All I need is an address."

"Don't look so panicked, little mouse," Liam said with a soft smile, giving her a quick hug before grabbing a cup of coffee. "I can drive you to work. We did invite you here after all."

Cammie breathed a sigh of relief and gave the location to Josie. It was a little strange to watch the two of them act so completely normal after the fantastic night they had exploring each other's bodies.

Cammie had woken with Josie's protective arms still wrapped around her.

"Thank you for taking care of me," Cammie said shyly.

Josie kissed Cammie's forehead in a very maternal manner, and Cammie inhaled the scent of her skin and soap, "You're always welcome here little one." They exchanged numbers before Cammie dragged Liam out the door, "Quickly, Daddy, I'm going to be late."

Chapter 4

Come over this weekend, little mouse. We have another surprise for you.

Cammie bit her lip as she stared down at her phone, reading the message from Liam a few times before attempting a reply, typing and retyping. They had spent every day for the last few days messaging back and forth. They had set a few ground rules for her, and in turn, she had told them what she would and would not do.

They had agreed, and so their friendship grew.

I'd love to, Daddy, but I can't. My friends are in town, and we're going out. Fingers trembling, she hastily added, *I promised them I would be there.*

Cammie was a nervous wreck. She didn't want Liam or Josie to be disappointed, especially not this early on in their relationship. They had just gotten to know each other, and she really liked them. Something of a feat these days.

Are you telling me or asking me, Cammie?

Her heart hammering, she quickly typed her reply just as her Manager came into the back office and looked at her reproachfully.

Please, can I go, Daddy? I can't break my promise. Pretty please?

Cammie hadn't had a chance to check her messages again until the end of her shift but was relieved to see that Liam had agreed to her going out after all.

Thank you, Daddy! Cammie added a heart and a smiley face as an added cuteness. It was late Friday night, and Cammie had planned to have a couple of drinks with her colleagues but thought better of it and drove herself home.

Cammie dropped her keys and her bag on the kitchen counter and headed straight for the fridge. She pulled out the day-old Chow Mein and threw it into the microwave. As her food heated up, Cammie looked longingly at the open bottle of wine on the counter. Josie had strictly disapproved of Cammie drinking any alcohol while they spent time together, and as she thought about pouring herself a small glass to help her wind down, a bubble of disapproval tickled in the pit of Cammie's stomach.

Cammie shrugged off the feeling of guilt and poured the rest of the bottle into a large wine glass. *Better to finish it and remove future temptation*, she thought. Cammie ate her leftovers in silence. She missed the closeness she had shared with Liam and Josie.

Another thought occurred to her as she threw back the last of the wine. She wouldn't really be able to message Liam or Josie while her friends were in town. She toyed with the idea of simply switching her phone off and dealing with the aftermath later but thought better of it. Feeling slightly buzzed, Cammie shot Liam a quick message:

I won't be able to message a lot while I'm with my friends, but I'll be a good girl.

***

Cammie had met her group of friends in college nearly ten years ago. They stayed in touch and met as often as varying schedules and geographical locations allowed. Today marked a sort of anniversary for the group, and as such, the day had been booked well in advance. Plans were made, and schedules were changed. Everyone was going to be there. All six of them.

Cammie had excitedly squashed herself into her car with five other bodies. They were loud. They were happy, and they had already started to drink. Normally, Cammie would be first to crack open a bottle of wine, but her conscience hounded her.

Liam, Josie, and Cammie had discussed this part of their agreement. In fact, they had discussed a couple of things, but they had wanted to ensure that Cammie looked after herself, even if they couldn't always be there.

They hadn't signed a contract, but there had to be some structure laid out to keep Cammie in line when she wasn't with them. She had made a promise to try and adhere to their rules. It was for her own good, she knew.

However, Cammie felt justified in her choices, given that she was still a grown adult capable of making her own choices.

Cammie was enjoying her evening but became visibly uncomfortable when they reached the bar, and her eyes fell on her ex. It hadn't ended amicably. He had been her Daddy, but later she learned he was in it only for the sex and nothing else. She had lost her trust in people. More importantly, she had started to hate that she needed to be taken care of.

"Hey, little girl." His drawl sent a shiver up her spine. "Shouldn't you be in bed by now?" The double meaning was crystal clear, and it turned her stomach. Kain knew which buttons to push to irritate her.

Liz, who had heard the entire exchange, hooked her arm through Cammie's and pushed through the crowd ahead of them. The force of jostling people out of the way had caused another patron to stumble over his already unsteady footing and spilled his drink over Kain.

As was the norm where alcohol flowed deep and emotions were left unchecked. A fistfight broke out.

The pair kept pushing through the crowd and disappeared among the writhing mass of hot bodies to where their friends were waiting with yet another tray of drinks. They seemed to have managed to recruit a waiter to serve them all night.

Cammie looked at the tray of shots in front of her. At the start of the evening, she had expressed her wish to avoid alcohol, claiming an early shift the next day. Now, however, as she came face to face with the pink, strawberry-flavored liqueur, her willpower faltered.

The echo of Josie's warning angered her this time. Why shouldn't she drink? It wasn't as if they were here. She was an adult. She kept reminding herself. With a bratty sort of stubbornness, she shot the liquid down her throat and tapped the glass on the table. The girls cheered and did the same.

Steadily, more shots and cocktails appeared on their table as well as in Cammie's hand. She had abandoned her conscience six drinks ago and was as loud and exuberant as her friends. They periodically returned to the dancefloor and jumped, gyrated, and threw their arms around as they lost themselves in the music and booze. Cammie felt relaxed and carefree.

There were no responsibilities at that moment; all that mattered was that she maintained her buzz.

It was close to four in the morning when they stumbled out of the club. Liz had called a cab, and they were waiting in the crisp early morning air for it to arrive. The rest had gone home hours ago.

Cammie waved and shouted greetings as Liz' cab pulled away, Liz hanging out of the window to wave back. When the cab disappeared around the corner, Cammie headed for her car.

The cool air had cleared her head a little, but it wasn't enough.

The warmth of the car and the fact that she had

started to calm down was making her head spin a little more. Her car swerved onto the sidewalk, nearly missing a trash can. Cammie slowed down but continued driving. Her mind focused on getting home and straight to bed.

It wasn't until the lights painted the world blue and the siren's whoop cut through the fog in her brain that Cammie realized she hadn't quite driven as straight as she initially thought. Or as slow.

Fuck.

Even though the fog in her head was clouding her judgment, she could imagine Liam and Josie's disappointed faces clearly. Cammie's stomach turned unhappily.

Over the sound system came the booming voice of God - or so Cammie thought it sounded - and asked her to put both her hands out of the window. She did as she was told. There was a click, and the seconds trickled by like molasses through the eye of a needle. Agonizingly slow. Her head was spinning, and a new kind of uneasiness settled in the pit of her stomach. One that had nothing to do with the fact that she had been pulled over.

"Ma'am, have you been drinking?" It was standard questions, but Cammie knew the officer hadn't needed to ask. The alcohol vapor was coming off of her in waves.

Cammie blinked at him, stupidly, "No?" Her lie was obvious, but she couldn't help it.

"Ma'am, please step out of the vehicle."

Cammie wanted to argue, but her brain was struggling with the concept. She slowly opened the door from the outside. The latch clicked, and then her stomach lurched.

Oh no. No.

Cammie pushed the door open and-

The officer had barely enough time to step back as the contents of her stomach splashed on the ground.

***

Cammie woke to the sound of metal clanging on metal. Her eyes were gummed shut, and her

mouth tasted like sewage. Her head pounded as she sat up carefully, too fragile to move too quickly. Nauseatingly bright light streamed through the high window, indicating that she had been there for most of the night.

The offending sound was coming from the slightly older-looking officer unlocking her cell, "Come on, time to sort this out."

The officer was polite and didn't touch her or talk too loud. He gave her a small smile, "We deal differently, miss. Just be sure this is what you want to be stuck with for the rest of your life."

Cammie stood close enough to read his name tag, or at least, after a few tries, she did manage to read it: Leo White successfully.

He indicated down the passage and stepped aside so that Cammie could get past him. Leo led her through the back of the station and set her down in front of a young officer that looked much too eager to be working this early in the morning, "Please wait right here, miss."

She sat in an uncomfortable chair, fidgeting. This

early on a Monday morning, there wasn't much activity, but she still felt as though a million eyes were on her. At least she wasn't handcuffed. Perhaps it was the utter look of defeat on her face or the fact that her short stature set them at ease. Whatever the reason, Cammie was grateful. She wasn't sure that her self-esteem could take a blow like that.

That is until Josie walked into the room. There was a flicker of recognition before the anger and disappointment set in. Cammie knew what she must've looked like: smeared mascara, disheveled, and she probably still smelled like stale smoke and booze. Sleeping it off in the drunk tank didn't exactly come with shower privileges.

Josie approached the desk and addressed the officer busy feeding her information into the system, "Who's representing her?"

"We're still processing her details. W-we haven't called-"

Cammie was glad that the look she gave him was not aimed in her direction, although she was sure there would be time enough for that later.

Josie looked over the docket that the now sweating officer had handed her. She went still. It was one thing to see Cammie in the police station, but to see those three letters inked onto the page caused anger to freeze her veins.

"No matter," Josie said, handing back the file. "I'll arrange for representation."

"Yes, ma'am." The officer, relieved that the irritation was short-lived, continued hammering the keys.

"Send her to my office once you are done. We'll read the charges when her lawyer gets here." When Josie looked at Cammie again, the anger had softened. It wasn't gone, but at least Cammie felt that she wasn't hated.

Josie had given Cammie some baby wipes to clean off her face, and some gum to help kill the gritty and gross feeling that lingered in her mouth.

When Liam had gotten the call from Josie, he could hardly believe it. First, he was furious. Then he started to think about what could have happened.

He stepped through the door on that early Monday morning, and his eyes searched for her.

A silence hung between the three of them. Cammie stared at her shoes, picking at her nails. The polish, showing a nervous habit, chipped and peeled in several places.

Liam tried to keep his voice low, and he did so by sheer force of will. It wouldn't do to yell at her. She had broken the rules. It wasn't even that. She had put herself and others at risk. He was torn between berating her as a lawyer and comforting her as her Daddy. But she had broken the rules, and she had to be punished. First, by the law - there was no way out of it - and then by Liam and Josie.

"I was stupid," Cammie said, still not looking at either of them.

"No," Josie interjected. "You may have done a stupid thing, but it doesn't mean you are stupid." Cammie had no reply.

Liam inhaled a deep breath and let it out slowly.

"Alright, so this is what's going to happen,"

Liam said and proceeded to run through the events as they would play out. "You will plead guilty, and then we will go to trial."

"What? Why?" Cammie looked up, surprised, and angry.

"You *are* guilty, Cammie," Liam stressed. "You could have hurt someone. You could have hurt yourself."

"Cammie, sweetheart. Something like this can't just be swept away. You need to understand that there will always be consequences for your actions." Josie's voice was kind but firm. Cammie looked at her as tears welled in her eyes and nodded.

"The plea hearing is in," Liam checked his watch, "three hours."

"I smell like a dirty ashtray and liquor; I can't show up like this. They've impounded my car." Cammie's voice was thick with emotion and anger.

"I slept in a jail cell and look like something the cat dragged in. How am I supposed to-"

Cammie abruptly stopped taking when the frustration brought on tears. She hadn't really hoped that she would get away with it, but faced with the sudden realization that she was in serious trouble had caused anxiety to knot painfully in the pit of her stomach.

Liam contemplated for a brief moment whether that would be fitting punishment but then chastised himself. She needed to face the consequences, not be humiliated. He sighed, "We'll get you cleaned up."

Josie called for Leo, and in the few moments that followed, the room was silent.

"Yes, ma'am?" Leo said.

"Could you kindly stand in as Miss Chase's police escort for the afternoon until her plea hearing?"

"Yes, ma'am." Leo beckoned to Cammie, "Ready when you are, Miss."

Cammie was silently grateful for the friendly face as he led her out of the building.

Leo had made polite conversation as they headed

down to her apartment in his police cruiser. Cammie had taken a quick shower, dressed in a black dress she wore for a formal work function, and at Josie's request packed a few extra things into her bag.

Cammie tried to keep it together. Her world was slowly falling apart around her. Maybe Kain had been right. Cammie felt as alone right now as she had the day he had called her a needy, bratty, slut, and walked out of her life.

"Are you okay, Miss?" Leo asked, his eyes crinkling with concern.

Cammie nodded, steeled herself, and locked her apartment door behind her. It would be tomorrow's problem.

***

"Do you have family in the city?"

"No, sir- Your Honor," Cammie corrected herself and felt her cheeks burn.

After a moment of deliberation, the Judge shuffled

the papers in front of him and called the council to the bench.

"Mr. Everhart, your client may have a job in the city, but since she has no relations or other ties here, I am inclined to keep her locked up until trial."

"Your Honor, I will personally see to it that she shows up to the hearing. She can post bail. She has no priors." Liam said quietly.

"With all due respect, counselor, your client is a danger to herself and others. She admitted guilt-"

"To making a mistake."

"Enough." The Judge held up his hand. "Mr. Everhart, can you with certainty say that the defendant will not fail to appear at her hearing?" Liam considered this. Cammie needed a firm hand, that was certain, but she had not proven to be the type to run away simply. She may have hated to be in a situation that she herself created, but Cammie had accepted the consequences as they were.

"Yes, your Honor."

"Will you take responsibility?"

"Yes, your honor."

The Judge peered at him with eyes that seemed to take in every inch of his soul, and with a wave of his hand, dismissed them.

The Judge addressed the room, and Liam noticed how Cammie's back straightened just a little.

"Guilty. Bail is set at a thousand-two-hundred dollars. Miss Chase, I am releasing you into Mr. Everhart's care. Sentencing is scheduled for ten days from today."

Chapter 5

The car ride home was painfully quiet. Cammie hadn't dared to say a word. It was one thing to disobey the rules set out by Liam and Josie, but it was quite another to break the law.

Cammie knew she had screwed up royally. In all honesty, she was waiting for Liam to drive her to her tiny apartment and leave her there, essentially nullifying their agreement.

She was still on probation with them. *Maybe not for long*, Cammie thought. Cammie wasn't keen on finding out where Liam and Josie stood with her, so she remained silent, listening to Liam breathe.

When they pulled up in front of Liam's house, Cammie looked at him in surprise, her mouth wanting to form words, but her brain refusing to supply them.

"Upstairs, now," Liam demanded, putting the car in park. "I'll be up in a minute. Josie is already waiting for us."

Cammie slid out of the car and let herself into the house, trying to make as little noise as possible. The front door was unlocked, and the interior was dead quiet. The bright light of the living room guiding her like a beacon in the storm. The second Cammie saw Josie with her back to the door. Her throat went dry.

Cammie stood awkwardly in the threshold between the living room and the kitchen, clutching her one arm close to her body. She heard the door close behind her, and Liam joined Josie in the kitchen.

Cammie could barely breathe as the stress gnawed at her, their eyes looking right through her.

"Cammie." It was all he had to say. Cammie knew there was going to be a discussion about the events of the past few days. The one thing that she hadn't shared with them was that she tended to lose control when alcohol was involved. It was a coping mechanism, a crappy one to be sure, but still. Liam and Josie were both standing in the kitchen, a chair had been pulled out for her, and they waited. Taking a deep breath, Cammie shuffled towards them and sat down. Her heart was in her throat, and her face was burning from shame.

"Cammie, what happened?" Cammie had expected Josie to be furious, shouting at her, but she wasn't. Her voice was calm, and Cammie thought, concerned.

Cammie had kept it together since the police station, but the second she opened her mouth to speak, the stress broke her. Cammie dropped her head in her hands and cried. Sobs wracked her whole body, shaking her, stealing the breath from her lungs, and causing her to sob harder.

Liam and Josie shared a look of concern. It seemed to them that Cammie had been holding on to whatever it was that was eating away at her.

Josie wrapped her arms around Cammie, letting the girl's tears drip and soak into her blouse, "Everything will be okay, honey. I promise."

Cammie sobbed harder, and for what seemed like

an eternity, Cammie clutched at Josie and cried from the depths of her soul. When her sobs quieted, and her body stopped shaking, Cammie wiped at her eyes and face and looked up at Josie's waiting form.

They still expected some kind of explanation, and Cammie knew, the punishment was non-optional.

Cammie took a steadying breath, and tested her voice, cleared her throat and tried again, "Are you mad at me?"

A brief pause.

"We were, little one, but only because we were scared." Josie reached out and wiped a stray tear from her face, "Mommy and Daddy want to help you, but you need to tell us everything, Cammie."

"Okay, Mommy."

And so, she did. Cammie told them what had happened, including the part about her vomiting over a police officer's shoes. Liam and Josie were respectful, listening to her whole story before they asked their next questions.

"Who is Kain?" Liam asked, a slight edge to his voice. The longer he listened to Cammie explain her past relationship and how Kain had treated her, the angrier he got. He kept it in check, however, and the whole mess was eventually unloaded.

Cammie had laid bare absolutely everything about herself to these two people. She was vulnerable but relieved. Now, she thought, it's up to them if they still want her or not.

"I'm sorry, Mommy. Daddy." Cammie was close to tears again, "I made a bad choice, and it got me into so much trouble, and I was worried this whole time that you would be too angry ever to want to talk to me again."

"Little mouse, we're not going to abandon you for making a mistake," Liam said, "but you have to own up to them."

"Everything you do has a consequence, Cammie," Josie said, her face serious, but the kindness never leaving her voice.

Cammie nodded mutely, still wiping tears from her

face.

"Cammie, you've been a bad girl," Josie said.

"Yes, Mommy."

"What did you do?"

"I broke the rules."

"Which rules did you break, Cammie?" Liam prompted.

Cammie swallowed, still feeling a little fragile, "I disobeyed Mommy."

"What else?"

"I drank alcohol, and I'm not allowed to," Cammie said. Once the words were out, the rest followed, "I drove a car while being drunk, and I put other people in danger. I lied, and I ignored messages from Mommy and Daddy." Cammie breathed shakily, but let everything flow out. It was cathartic in a way, to come clean. Confessing her sins and secrets had released a part of her, she hadn't realized she was holding on to.

"That's right," Josie said.

"What happens when you break the rules, little mouse?"

Cammie looked at the two of them where they stood in the kitchen and felt a warmth spread through her. She knew she messed up, but they weren't angry at her. She had disappointed them, but they did not shout or raise their voices. They allowed her to tell her story, her version of events, not the black and white paragraphs of the docket, and they were still kind towards her.

"I get punished."

"Do you understand why we have to punish you?" Josie asked. Cammie nodded. Their caring manner made her feel less like a failure and more like someone who simply needed proper guidance. Her vulnerability was exposed, and Cammie waited. Liam and Josie were exactly the kind of people she needed in her life. They could provide her the stability she so desperately needed. Cammie knew she needed a firm hand. Liam and Josie knew that too.

"Use your big girl words, Cammie." Liam prompted, his voice still low.

"Yes, Mommy." Cammie finally answered

Josie's question.

"Good girl. Now, follow Daddy, please."

Liam held out his hand to Cammie, and she took it, grateful for the contact. She followed him to a room up another flight of stairs. It was pleasantly decorated but had chains attached to the bed, along with a wall-mounted display of whips, paddles, and other paraphernalia. Cammie swallowed.

Liam led her to the bed and told her to bend over. She was still dressed in the modest dress she wore for the hearing.

She did as Liam asked, and he lifted the hem of her dress over her bottom, exposing the pink undies she had bought on the day they had run into each other.

He had made a show of choosing a large, wooden paddle. It was thick and had etchings carved into the handle. Liam placed the cool wood against Cammie's ass and held it there for a time. Cammie quivered in anticipation.

Liam did not ask her to count this time.

Whack.

Whack. Whack. Whack.

After a few harder blows, Liam would pause to run the paddle against her bottom. He didn't say a word as he punished her. Cammie had started to squirm and squeak softly as the blows landed.

"Daddy?" Cammie asked when a particularly hard hit caused her eyes to water, "Daddy, can we stop, please?"

Again, Liam did not speak, but he did set the paddle down to stroke Cammie's ass. He slid her panties down, and the coolness of the air against her skin brought a moment of relief. Cammie let out a shaky breath.

"Stand up, little one," Liam commanded, and Cammie obeyed, her eyes wide. Liam smiled reassuringly, "You'll be okay, little mouse."

"Remember, we'll stop when you tell us to," Josie said.

Cammie nodded. Her eyes were still wide, but she trusted them. Cammie had been asked to undress. She did so while both Liam and Josie watched.

"Come here, little girl." Josie held out a set of thick, leather cuffs, with a very short chain between them. "Turn around."

Cammie did and held perfectly still, and Josie cuffed her arms together behind her back, "Good girl."

Liam had exchanged the paddle for a thin spanking whip with a flared tip. Josie had gently made Cammie bend over the bed again, her ass in the air, legs apart.

When the first blow landed, Cammie let out a squeak of surprise. It hadn't hurt nearly as much as she had anticipated, but the thin leather felt very different from the wooden paddle she was used to.

Liam made her count. One, loud, hard, *whack* for every day of her sentence. By the time the thirtieth spank came around, Cammie was panting. Both from the pain and the pleasure of it.

"Do you understand why you're being punished, baby girl?" Liam asked as he loosened his tie.

"Yes, Daddy. I'm sorry, Daddy."

Josie took the opportunity to work a small, silicone butt plug into her ass hole. Cammie squirmed and voiced her distress at having something penetrating her there.

"You know the words to make us stop, little girl. Any time it gets too much." Liam whispered in her ear as he stood in front of Cammie, his cock hard and standing at attention.

"Open your mouth, Cammie."

Liam wrapped his fingers through her hair and held her steady as she sucked on his dick.

Cammie jerked in surprise as a thick cock spread her pussy lips so far apart that she felt as though she was going to break in two. She pulled away from Liam and strained to see behind her. Josie had a thick dildo strapped onto her and was slowly working its thick head into her already soaked pussy.

Cammie came multiple times as both Liam and Josie stretched her to her limits. Still, she did not protest. Even though some of it hurt, Cammie felt safe enough to know that they would not seriously hurt her.

***

Liam undid the straps on the cuffs around Cammie's wrists, gently massaging blood flow back into her arms and fingers, "How do you feel, Cammie?"

"I-" Cammie paused, mentally running a hand over her body and assessing her emotions. "I'm sore, Daddy."

"What can I do to make my little girl feel better?" Liam asked, still running his fingers over her wrists and arms.

"I want a hug," Cammie said, "and a bubble bath."

"How about a warm bottle and cuddles while we watch some TV after?" Liam suggested as he effortlessly lifted Cammie onto his lap. Cammie sank into his body, absorbing the warmth and closeness of her Daddy's touch.

Liam rocked her gently, listening to her breathing. When she was ready, Cammie pulled away slightly and asked him to carry her to her bathroom, where Josie had already prepared a hot bubble bath for her.

"Would you like Mommy to bathe you, or me?" Liam asked as he set the girl down on the toilet seat.

"Mommy," Cammie said as she reached up for Josie.

"What do we say?" Liam prompted.

"Please, will you stay with me, Mommy?"

"Of course, my sweetheart," Josie said. Liam closed the door behind them, listening to the girls' chatter and splash as they cleaned up.

By the time they had finished, Liam had already made a giant pile of blankets and pillows on the living room floor. Josie and Cammie made themselves comfortable, snuggling close together. Liam was surprised by how different Cammie was compared to the other Littles they had cared for. She seemed to require more physical touch while some others preferred a quick cuddle and alone time.

"Here you go, little mouse," Liam said and handed her a baby bottle filled with strawberry flavored milk.

"Thank you, Daddy." Cammie said and snuggled into Josie's heavy chest, "Can we please watch My Little Pony?"

"Whatever you want, little mouse."

And that's how they spent the remainder of the night. Cammie snuggled between Liam and Josie, as she animatedly described each of the characters and their backstories in great detail.

The show was still running when Cammie had fallen asleep with her head on Liam's chest. Not wanting to disturb her, Liam and Josie had simply stayed with her, talking quietly as the colorful ponies went on their friendship adventures.

Chapter 6

The following morning Liam had taken Cammie to work. Her car had been impounded, and since he was responsible for the girl until her hearing, it only made sense that he drive her.

Cammie's mood had only marginally improved. She shifted uncomfortably in the passenger seat. Her bottom was still tender after the punishment last night.

"Thank you, Daddy, for driving me to work again."

"It's no trouble, sweetheart."

***

Josie had been going over Cammie's paperwork, ensuring that the docket was as complete as possible. All new information had been fed into the system and added to her file. Josie looked up from her papers just as Liam rapped a knuckle on the doorframe of her office, "Got a minute?"

"Anything for you, Liam." Her smile was genuine, and he shut the door behind him, "Is there something specific I can help with, or is this a social call?" The playful twinkle in Josie's eyes told him she didn't make a distinction between the two.

The woman was insatiable. With a returning grin, he said, "Definitely not the time or place, Josie." They shared a laugh as he kissed her cheek, half-falling, half-sitting in the old gray couch across the desk.

"It's about Cammie," he said. "I think the girl needs-" he paused to find just the right word, "more permanent supervision."

Josie didn't look at all surprised at his suggestion, "Permanently? As in, permanently with us?"

"Yes."

"What if she isn't interested, Liam?"

"Look at how well she responded to us last night, Josie. She needs structure and permanence."

"I agree that she needs the structure," Josie said and leaned forward in her chair, swiveling closer to him, "but we need to be sure that it is what she would want. We can't force her, no matter the dynamic between us. She's still a fully grown adult."

Liam took in her words. Josie was right, of course, but that didn't mean he wasn't going to try. He told Josie exactly that, and they began discussing the details.

"There's one more thing we need to consider here, Liam," Josie said seriously, "We need to consider the possibility that Cammie wouldn't agree to any of this."

"I am aware of that, Josie."

"I want to take care of her, too, Liam." There was a long moment of silence as Liam mulled over her words, and his mind worked through multiple scenarios.

"How about a trial run, then?" Josie finally said.

Liam sat forward, suddenly a little more lively, "It

would be perfect. You're a genius, Josie."

"It's why you married me," Josie said with a wink.

***

At the end of Cammie's shift, she found Liam already in the parking lot waiting for her. She waved excitedly and hopped in the passenger side, "Hi, Daddy!"

"Hi, little mouse. How was your day?" Cammie took off, talking about the job, the people, and the customers. When Cammie noticed that her voice was getting to be a little louder than she had intended, she stopped short and lowered her voice, "Sorry, Daddy."

"Do you hate your job?" Liam asked, not wanting her to stop talking yet.

"I don't really hate it, but it just drains me sometimes, you know?" Cammie stared ahead and watched the light change from red to green. As Liam pulled away, she added, "I do sometimes like it, but it's not what I had wanted to do for this long. It was just supposed to be a stepping stone."

"Have you thought about quitting?"

"I can't really afford to even if I wanted to," Cammie said honestly. She had debts and rent. Not to mention, the bail money she had paid had left a giant hole in her bank account, which was yet another thing she would need to worry about.

"What would you like to do?" Liam asked probing. Cammie thought for a moment, and a smile broke over her face. *She really is a lovely girl*, Liam thought as he stole glances. Cammie spent the greater part of the ride home talking about her dreams.

Liam made the appropriate noises for her to continue the conversation, but otherwise, simply let her talk. The passion he saw burning in her eyes made him absolutely certain that Cammie would be great with the two of them.

"Josie and I want to discuss something with you," Liam said as they pulled up to the house, and Cammie's story came to a close.

"What is it?"

"Let's go inside. We can discuss it there."
Cammie threw her arms around Josie as she stepped into the living room, inhaling her warm scent. She felt safe here.

"We know you have a lot going on at the moment, Cammie. Especially after the latest developments."
Cammie cringed at the memory, and her stomach turned. *I am never drinking again.* "It's been a little hectic," she agreed.

"What is it?" Cammie asked, seeing him hesitate.

"Please, understand that you shouldn't feel obligated in any way," Josie said.

"We want you to move in with us. Permanently." Liam offered.

***

Cammie had accepted their offer without much thought. She hated living alone but could never quite bring herself to get a roommate.

In a short amount of time, they had gone from strangers to friends to family. Cammie could hardly believe her luck. Here she was, a college dropout, finding her place with two of the most amazing humans she knew.

They had already shared so much of themselves with each other, both physically and mentally. Cammie didn't have to think about it, because she knew it was what she had been looking for.

It took just one day for Cammie to have her apartment cleared out and her things brought over. The three of them sat at the kitchen counter with a stack of paperwork in front of them. It took a while as they worked through each part of the document Liam had drawn up.

Whatever wasn't understood was explained and rephrased to make the meaning clear. The document covered everything from her chosen safe words, fantasies, and triggers down to public displays and outright bondage.

They had set out the ground rules and the punishments attached should they be broken. Cammie agreed with most and asked for changes to be made to some things that she hadn't quite yet felt comfortable with.

This led to the creation of a detailed list of her personal limits. Some, like participating in anal sex was a soft limit for her, while others such as blood play were completely off the table.

Cammie agreed to wear whatever they chose for her outside of her work uniform. For the duration of her community service, she would be forced to wear a butt plug and diaper at all times unless express permission was given for removal.

In turn, they each signed the contract once they were satisfied with its contents.

Cammie felt giddy. It was the start of something great.

Chapter 7

Liam, Josie, and Cammie stood in the doorway of the spare bedroom, looking at the empty space. The three of them had cleared out the furniture and decorations in preparation for Cammie moving in with them.

"Can we paint one wall egg-shell blue?" Cammie asked as she saw Josie hold up what looked like paint samples against the stark white walls.

"Maybe, but let's see what other colors we have, too," Josie said and beckoned Cammie over. Together they looked through the stack of color tabs.

"What about this one?" Josie prompted. It was a light green. The label said it was a lime milkshake color, but Cammie giggled and shook her head.

"Noooo," Cammie said adamantly.

"Why not?" Josie said, surprised by Cammie's reaction.

"It looks like a nose boogie," Cammie whispered conspiratorially, still giggling.

"Cammie!" Josie scolded but laughed. She had to agree. The color was definitely not as nice as it had seemed a few minutes ago. Josie discarded the color tab and lined up the remaining five.

And so they worked their way through their final choices and settled on two. A sunshine yellow (which Cammie was so excited about that she nearly ran Liam over when they went to show him) and a dark, muted purple. They also decided to use a light gray as an accent color.

Cammie had spent the week practicing how to draw a mouse and went to show Josie when she finally managed to make it look the way she had wanted it to.

"Mommy?" Cammie asked as Josie looked over the drawing Cammie had given her.

"Yes, my sweet?"

"Can-can I paint that on my wall?"

Cammie had expected Josie to deny her request outright, but by the smile on her face, Cammie felt hope rise and bubble in her chest.

"Do you want me to help, or can you do it by yourself?"

"I'm- I'm allowed to paint by myself?" Cammie asked incredulously.

"Yes, you adorable little mouse," Josie said and hugged her tightly. "It's your room, and we can decorate it however you want."

***

Cammie stood enthralled in front of the wall of plushies. Her eyes darted from one plushie to the other. The colors were overwhelming, and she found herself touching each one, feeling the fur under her fingertips.

"Mommy?" Cammie said softly, tugging on the hem of her blouse.

"Yes, sweetheart?" Josie had been watching

her as the girl took in every detail. She could see the twinkle of sheer joy in her eyes as they darted from one fuzzball to the next.

"I don't know which one to choose." Her voice was small and sounded as though it was about to break.

"It's okay, Cammie," Josie reassured her and squeezed her shoulders. "Take your time."

"Okay, Mommy." Cammie's tension drifted away, and she started picking up plushies and holding them to her. After some time passed, she would either place them in a pile at her feet or return them to the shelf. Josie watched, her heart filling with joy.

"Are you having fun, little one?" Josie asked. Cammie was distracted as she stared intently at the plushie in her hands. It was a gray mouse as big as her torso and nearly as wide. It was fat and round, with small pink hands and feet.

When the girl had made up her mind, she spun to face Josie, her eyes full of tears, "I want this one!" Cammie was shaking. The stuffie was large, soft, and cute. Her heart was breaking at the thought of Josie saying no, and she could barely keep her tears in check.

"Are you sure, little girl?"

Cammie nodded vigorously, causing some of her butterfly clips to come undone. Josie wrapped her arm around the girl and pulled her close, kissing the top of her head, "Go show Daddy, little one."

Cammie was off like a rocket. She found him only two aisles over where he was measuring the size of a very large bed with rails made of thick wood. It stood high off of the ground and looked to be hand-carved. A small ladder attached to each side allowed the user to climb into the bed comfortably.

"Daddy, look!" Cammie held the fat stuffie in front of his face, "It's a mouse! Isn't he cute?"

Liam gasped and dramatically held his heart, "Goodness! A mouse for my little mouse."

Cammie giggled and held the stuffie close to her chest as if she was afraid that someone would make her return it to its place on the shelf.

"Why don't you go give it to the cashier by

the front counter?" Liam suggested. Cammie hesitated, but Liam smiled, the softness of the action crinkling the corners of his eyes, "We have to pay for it, darling. The cashier can ring it up in the meantime. You don't have to leave it there."

The kindly cashier nodded in her direction, and Cammie did as Liam had said. Cammie felt her heart thump wildly in her chest as the cashier handed the fat mouse back to her after just a few seconds.

"So, I can keep this?" Cammie asked the man.

"Of course, little one," Josie said as she dropped off a handful of colorful sheets. "These as well, thank you, Ed."

"No problem, Ms. Josie."

Cammie shouted in elation and whizzed away, running through the aisles to look at the rest of the things the store had to offer.

***

"There you are!" Josie called. Cammie was quietly sitting in one of the small plastic chairs in the corner as Liam and Josie had gone about their shopping spree. Cammie had lost interest after the first hour.

"I got tired, Mommy," Cammie said, still clutching her new stuffie.

"It's okay, little girl. Let's go home."

***

When Cammie returned from work the next day, Liam had already installed the crib, and the room was lit by soft lighting coming from a lamp on a matching end table.

"Woooow." Cammie breathed. The room looked exactly like she had imagined. She saw that Josie had carefully placed Meekie on her pillow as if it were waiting for Cammie to return home.

"What do you think, Cammie?" Liam asked as he stood in the doorway, watching her admire the room.

"I love it, Daddy." Cammie threw her arms around him, pressing herself against his already hardening cock.

"Daddy?" Cammie asked, her eyes dark with heat

"Yes, little one?"

"I want you to touch me, Daddy," Cammie said, taking his hand and pressing it firmly between her legs. She rubbed herself against his fingers, "When will Mommy be home? I want her to be here too."

As if on cue, they heard keys jangle in the lock.

"Mommy!"

Cammie ambushed Josie before she had made it halfway across the living room, "I want us to play together, Mommy."

Josie met Liam's gaze, saw the bulge in his pants, and grinned, "Ambushed you first?"

Liam laughed and nodded.

"Well, then, little girl. Why don't you come help Mommy change into something more comfortable?" Josie said, pulling her along by the hand.

"You should come too, Daddy," she added and winked at Liam.

Chapter 8

Cammie had chosen the same dress she had worn for her plea hearing. It was also quite possibly the only modest dress she owned, which made getting ready that morning pretty straightforward. Despite being ready to leave an hour before they were scheduled to show, Cammie had nervously straightened her dress and messed with her hair.

In the car, she couldn't sit still, fidgeting as Liam drove them to see the courthouse.

It wouldn't be a big trial that involved a jury, at least, and for that, Cammie was grateful. So far, she had managed to keep her private life private, especially from her employers. It would be horrifying if she lost her job because of something she could have prevented.

It was the same Judge they had seen for the plea hearing. He looked as surly as ever, and Cammie took a steadying breath.

The charges against Cammie were laid out, and in turn, the sentencing was discussed. Liam had discussed with her the potential outcomes of the hearing today. From best case scenario to worst. Cammie had become pale when he explained to her that the chance existed that she could be sentenced to time behind bars.

Without getting her hopes up, Liam had also discussed with her the reasonable expectations given that it was a first-time offense. Cammie had only nodded, unable to speak.

Now, however, while they were arguing back and forth, Cammie had a host of questions bubbling up inside of her, making her heart pound loudly in her ears. Cammie knew there was no point in asking them now. What would happen would happen.

"Your Honor," Liam interjected, "The officers had no valid reason to pull her over. They didn't follow the procedure. My client's sobriety wasn't tested before they took her into custody."

"She was driving erratically, Your Honor." Liam's opponent all but shouted and stomped his foot like a petulant child. Cammie could see the vein in his neck throbbing. The opposition was going out of his way to get an extended sentence for her, and perhaps even jail time. Liam was flouting his every argument and laying out his own.

The Judge, to his credit, was listening intently. Cammie, on the other hand, couldn't help her mind wandering. She knew she ought to be paying attention, but the nervous energy kept her from hearing much over the buzz in her ears.

The room had gone quiet, which snapped Cammie back to reality. The Judge was looking at her as if he was waiting for a response to a question. The look on Liam's face sent a chill down his spine. She wasn't helping his case by not paying attention.

"Miss Chase?" The Judge looked annoyed, and Cammie swallowed.

"I'm sorry, Your Honor, I didn't quite catch the question," Cammie said, avoiding Liam's gaze, feeling her face burn.

"Are you willing to accept full responsibility

for your actions, Miss Chase?" The Judge repeated. Cammie did look at Liam then and saw him give her the slightest of nods. "Yes, Your Honor."

"Mr. Everhart has set up quite the compelling defense. However," he shuffled through his notes. He stared down at something through his tiny spectacles balancing on the tip of his nose, "the fact remains that you *were* operating a motor vehicle while under the influence of alcohol. The blood tests confirm that allegation despite improper procedures."

Cammie waited quietly for the Judge to continue.

"It is not a matter we take lightly, Miss Chase, and neither should you. While no major damage was done, you put others at risk through your selfish actions."

"Yes, Your Honor." Dread settled in her stomach. Perhaps she was going to go to jail after all.

"After reviewing your case, I am sentencing you to thirty days community service. I am also ordering you to attend Alcoholics Anonymous meetings during the same time period."

That was it: no gavel, no ceremony, and no more arguments. The Judge shoved the papers into a binder, set it aside, and motioned for the bailiff to bring forward the next case.

Liam guided Cammie out of the courtroom, his face unreadable. He cordially shook the hand of his opponent, and they went their separate ways. Cammie and Liam returned to his car. Again, the ride home was made in silence.

***

Cammie had taken the day off work to attend the sentencing hearing. Liam had dropped her off at home and with a reassuring hug, returned to work. She wandered aimlessly through the house, frustrated. As part of the deal, Josie had removed any and all alcohol from the house. She needed to take the edge off. Cammie had scoured every inch of the house before falling into the couch with a loud sigh.

Cammie was ashamed. At last, the realization hit her. *I need to make some permanent changes in my life,* Cammie thought. Time passed slowly, but Cammie remained on the couch, eventually drifting off to sleep.

When she woke, Cammie felt better and prepared for Liam and Josie's return by taking a bath. A bubble bath never failed to lighten her mood.

***

Liam and Josie had called a family meeting, and as before, the three of them sat at the kitchen counter.

"Liam told me how the hearing went," Josie said. "Which means, now we need to work out a new schedule for you, so you have enough time to do your chores."

"Yes, Mommy."

"Cammie, do you know how lucky you were in that courtroom today?" Liam asked, his gaze intense, and his lips drawn together tightly.

Cammie shook her head. Cammie was aware that she could have gone to jail for a few months but hadn't truly grasped how easily the Judge could have swung that way.

"Adams is spectacular at his job, and if he were facing off against anyone else, you could very well have ended up in the worst-case scenario, little one. You came off fairly light, given who we were up against today."

Cammie's eyes grew wide, "I didn't know, Daddy."

"Which is why, Josie and I think that in order for you to truly understand how serious we are about you following the rules, we will be giving you our own version of punishment."

Cammie grimaced and hugged her stuffie tighter. The fat little mouse had become a source of comfort to her that eased the ache of anxiety she felt when dealing with real-world problems.

"What are you going to do?" she asked.

"Starting right now, you will wear diapers and a butt plug every day."

"A what?" Cammie's voice was shrill. The

protest was more from disbelief than not understanding.

"Excuse me?"

Cammie mumbled an apology.

"You need to prove to us that you can be a good girl," Josie said.

"I *am* a good girl, Mommy."

Liam held up his hand and continued, "If you break more rules, the butt plug will stay in. If you obey the rules and prove that you are a good girl, we can take it out at night."

"And if we feel you aren't taking this seriously enough, the size of the butt plug will increase," Josie added.

"Do you understand, little mouse?"

Cammie nodded, then, "I understand, Daddy."

Chapter 9

The three of them had the following day off together. It was so rare that they hadn't quite realized it until Josie shot out of bed to attempt to wake Cammie for work. The clock read 8:39 AM. Cammie was sure to be late, even if she skipped breakfast.

"Cammie, honey, it's time to get up." Josie coaxed.

A tired and annoyed grumble made Josie climb into the bed with her. She crawled under the covers and gave Cammie a giant hug, stroking her hair.

"Come, little one. You'll be late."

Bleary-eyed, Cammie turned her head to look at Josie, "I don't have to get up today, Mommy."

"What about work? You'll get in trouble." Josie said firmly.

Cammie giggled softly, turned around completely,

and snuggled up to Josie. It was warm and comfortable, and Josie smelled nice.

"I don't have work today." Cammie yawned and fell right back asleep.

Josie lay there for a moment, silently laughing at herself. With a sigh of relief, Josie made to get up, but Cammie had wrapped her arms around her tightly, making small noises of protest with each attempt to dislodge them.

Josie surrendered and fell asleep. She only woke much later to the smell of cooking bacon. Her stomach grumbled, and she heard a muffled giggle. Josie opened her eyes to find Cammie staring at her, her hand in front of her mouth to silence her giggles.

"I'm sorry, Mommy. I didn't mean to wake you, but your tummy made me giggle so much."

"Is it growling again?" Josie asked in mock annoyance, rolling her eyes for added effect.

Cammie giggled again just as another loud gurgle spoke up from beneath the sheets.

"I can hear you two giggling in there," Liam

called. "Better come get some breakfast before I eat it all, even the pancakes."

Cammie let out a loud shout and flailed, almost falling from the bed.

"Careful, little one. You could get hurt." Josie steadied her and helped her get down.

Cammie giggled hysterically as she ran ahead, "I want pancakes, Daddy!"

***

Cammie had stubbornly attempted to help them clean up, despite Liam stopping her. Cammie had grabbed her plate and ran to the sink. She lost her footing and dropped the plate. It shattered with a loud crash.

Cammie stood among the mess, her heart hammering in her chest. She burst into tears, sinking to her knees, "I'm sorry, I'm sorry, please don't be mad."

"Cammie, I told you not to." Liam's voice was deep and heavy. Cammie's heart shrank, and she cried harder.

They got the mess cleaned up, and when Cammie had calmed down, Josie had punished her for disobeying Liam. As usual, the punishment turned into play and eventual sexual release for all three.

"Come, sweet little girl," Josie whispered as she held her hand out for Cammie. Josie had already loosened her bonds and was helping her stand. Cammie's footing was unsteady, and her eyes held a glazed, faraway look that pleased her.

Josie helped Cammie to her adjoining bathroom and sat her down on the toilet seat. They murmured about her punishment and the play that followed.

Cammie looked at her knees and listened to the running water. When the temperature was just right, Josie kissed the top of Cammie's head, "Let's get you cleaned up."

Cammie hopped into the bath, sinking into the bubbles. Her bottom still stung a little, but the water was soothing. Cammie was spent. Emotionally and physically.

"Mommy?"

"Yes, Cammie?"

"You can get in with me," Cammie offered. She could still see Josie's juices leaking from her swollen pussy. "The water is nice and warm."

"Do you think we'll both fit?" Josie asked, laughing slightly.

"Yes, Mommy!" Cammie splashed some water as she pulled her legs to her chest. Cammie wiggled excitedly as Josie stepped into the bath. There really was enough space for the two of them to sit comfortably.

After some time had passed, Cammie grabbed the large bottle of bath gel and held it out to Josie, "Please help me wash, Mommy."

"Alright. Turn around, baby."

Cammie shifted and tried to turn around too quickly, more water splashed out, causing the bathroom mat to get soaked, "Oops." Cammie giggled and finally managed to have her back facing Josie, with only a small amount of water making it onto the floor this time.

Josie glooped a sizable amount of body wash onto Cammie's duck-shaped bath sponge. Josie washed the girl's back and shoulders. When she was done, she made Cammie stand in the bath.

"Hold onto the hand railing, okay?" Josie reminded her.

"Yes, Mommy." Cammie dutifully held onto the safety rail and stood firmly, careful not to shift her weight suddenly and lose her footing. Standing in the tub was dangerous, and with the added slipperiness of the bubble bath only added to the danger.

Josie washed from the small of her back, running the sponge over Cammie's ass. She saw the redness was fading but was still gentle as she ran the sponge over the area again. Then Josie ran her hand between the girl's legs. Cammie shivered, and Josie noted the way her thighs quickly pressed together before she allowed her to continue.

Cammie was still sensitive to touch after Liam's punishment. Her body remembered the sensation, and she felt new moisture between her legs.

Whether Josie noticed or not, she never let on. She simply continued scrubbing.

Josie scrubbed Cammie's thighs and legs, then rinsed her off with the sponge and water. Cammie carefully turned around, still holding onto the safety rail. Josie refreshed the bath gel on the sponge and stood.

Josie lathered soap over Cammie's shoulders and arms, washing between each fold of her fingers and under her arms. She gently scrubbed around, under, and over Cammie's firm breasts. They were just enough for a handful. Cammie's nipples hardened under Josie's touch, but she kept scrubbing.

Josie sat back down in the bathtub. With one hand, she held onto Cammie's hip, and with the other, she lightly ran the sponge over her nether lips. The girl was clean-shaven, just the way Josie liked. It was a perk that Cammie had preferred it that way too.

Cammie's body was getting used to the sensation of the sponge and Josie's touch. It no longer quivered in anticipation, and Cammie sighed a silent sigh of relief. She wasn't sure if she would have been able to take any more torture.

Cammie sat down and lifted her one foot then the other. Josie scrubbed both, tickling her toes in the process. Cammie laughed and squirmed. More water splashed out. Liam knocked on the door and peeked inside, a hand over his eyes.

"How are my two favorite girls?" He asked.

"Mommy is tickling my feet!" Cammie laughed and squirmed some more.

"We're super, Liam," Josie said, smiling at how silly he looked with his hands over his eyes.

"I was thinking," Liam said, grinning, "we should have waffles and ice cream for dinner."

Cammie was exuberant, "Yes, please, yes please, yes please!"

Josie laughed, "Apparently, that's a yes."

"Excellent. You two have fun, I'll get started on those waffles." With that, Liam closed the door, and they were left alone again.

Liam and Josie laughed as Cammie licked her plate clean, strawberry syrup, and melted ice cream smeared on her nose and one of her cheeks.

"Silly goose," Josie said and wiped Cammie's face with a cloth.

Liam cleared up the kitchen while Josie and Cammie, her belly stuffed full of waffles and ice cream, waddled to her nursery.

Cammie, with some effort and a boost from a chuckling Josie, hoisted herself up onto her bed. It also functioned as a crib, but Cammie only needed it when she slept restlessly.

"Can I have some cuddles?" Cammie asked as she hugged her stuffed mouse, Meekie, to her chest. Her eyes were growing a little heavy, but she didn't want to fall asleep yet. She needed the comfort Josie gave her and was afraid that Josie would get up as soon as she fell asleep.

"Sure thing, sweetheart." Josie hopped onto the bed with Cammie and took up position behind her, pulling her in tight. Josie squished her while Cammie laughed and squirmed.

"Alright, little one. Time to settle down now." Josie pulled a blanket over her and tucked her in, making sure that Meekie's head was outside of the blanket.

"Don't let Meekie suffocate, okay?"

"I won't." Cammie gave a great yawn and settled in as Josie wrapped her arms around her bundled form. She stroked her hair and hummed quietly.

"Mommy?"

"Yes, little one?"

"Thank you for being my Mommy," Cammie said and snuggled closer.

Josie felt a lump in her throat and squeezed the girl tighter, "Thank you for letting me, Cammie."

It wasn't long before their evening's activities caught up with them, and they fell asleep. Liam came to check on them. He stood in the doorway for a long while, just watching them sleep.

"Good night, little mouse," he whispered as

he tucked a strand of hair behind her ear. Both his girls were fast asleep as he pulled the door behind him. He left it open a crack.

Chapter 10

On her first day of community service, Cammie had stopped by the Community Center to get her job assigned for that day. Each day was the same. Go to the center, get her assignment for the day, and carry on with her job.

When her service had started, Liam had insisted that she keep wearing the diaper and butt plug, reminding her of the conditions attached.

Cammie had occasionally taken it out when her shift had started, and then replaced it once her shift had ended before Liam came to collect her from work. So far, she had been careful and hadn't been caught. Cammie felt her heart race each time she took the butt plug out and stuffed it into her bag before starting her community service, or her shift at work. She knew Liam and Josie would be upset if they ever found out, but it was too big for her to get used to.

She had been helping out in the soup kitchen all of last week, and she had had time to replace it before Liam would arrive to collect her.

Today, however, Liam had arrived early.

When he saw her, Liam noticed a slight change in her behavior. Cammie looked decidedly uneasy, and, a little guilty.

At first, Liam thought it was simply because he had arrived earlier than normal. Cammie had politely requested that he remain in his car at the end of her community service shift. Cammie hadn't wanted to be seen as a 'little rich girl.'

Liam was grateful that Cammie was attempting to socialize with the other people around her. It would be good to learn from their experiences. None of the other people in her group had done anything too serious, all misdemeanors, and all minors.

If Cammie was seen being picked up and dropped off in a large, pricey SUV, the other people in her group could turn hostile. Liam was familiar with the dynamic. He could see her point and had agreed.

Liam actually had a different motive for arriving earlier. He wanted to check in on her progress with her supervisor. As part of her agreement with the court, as well as with him, was that she would take this situation seriously.

Second chances didn't happen frequently.

The other court-mandated punishment was that Cammie had to attend Alcoholics Anonymous. Her emotional wellbeing was a top priority, and being sure that she was giving it her all would set his mind at ease.

There was no doubt that Cammie was taking it seriously. However, the girl had a tendency to revert to old habits. It was easier to just fall back on doing the bare minimum in order to get by.

The new ground rules, as set out by their contract, enforced her full cooperation in legal matters. While Cammie was finishing up her shift, Liam and her supervisor chatted freely.

Cammie tried to keep her face neutral when Liam greeted her, "How's my girl?"

"I'm fine."

Liam arched a brow at her, "Excuse me?"

"I'm sorry, Daddy. I'm okay. I'm just a little tired."

"Alright." Liam wrapped an arm around her and gave her a side hug, "How about we stop for some ice cream on the way home, little mouse?"

The cloud behind her eyes broke, and she smiled, "Could we, please?"

Liam laughed as he opened the passenger door for her and helped her in, "Of course, little mouse."

The zipper on Cammie's bag hadn't been closed all the way, and as Cammie tossed it into the back seat, it fell on its side, allowing some of the contents to spill out. Cammie had been careless.

Cammie bounced excitedly in her seat, the dread of having her secret discovered forgotten, "Can I get more than one flavor, Daddy?"

Liam reached back to set it right side up to keep more things from flying out and saw it. Carefully wrapped in toilet paper was the large purple heart butt plug. Josie had chosen that one specifically for her.

As they reached the fast-food joint, Liam stopped the car in the parking lot, "Cammie, look at me."

"Yes, Daddy?" Cammie asked, still excited about the prospect of ice cream, looking at him expectantly.

"Were you a good girl today?"

A heartbeat.

"Yes, Daddy." Cammie's eyes were still wide with excitement, unaware that Liam had found the butt plug.

"Is there something you'd like to tell me, Cammie?"

"No, Daddy."

"Are you sure?"

"Yes, Daddy." Her voice was softer now, and she had some trouble maintaining eye contact. Her face burned with embarrassment.

Liam reached behind him and pulled the ball of toilet paper from the bag and held it out to her.

"Do you know what this is, little mouse?"

"No, Daddy."

Liam's eyes darkened, "Cammie, we have talked about lying. You know how I feel about it."

"Yes, Daddy."

Liam let the silence settle, wanting to see how far Cammie would go with her little game of pretend. Cammie refused to meet his gaze, squirming uncomfortably in her seat. Liam unfolded the little package. Slowly. Making sure Cammie saw every single move as he revealed the sparkly purple butt plug.

Cammie looked up at him from beneath her lashes. There was no way out of this now. Her face burned hotter, and her stomach churned.

"Is this yours, little mouse?"

"Yes, Daddy."

"Why aren't you wearing it?"

"It was uncomfortable, Daddy."

"Are you allowed to take it out?"

"No, Daddy."

Again Liam let the silence press in on them in the car. He could hear her strangled breathing and noted the tremble of her fingers as she laced and unlaced them in her lap. Liam placed the butt plug in her lap, and he started the car.

"Wait, Daddy!" Cammie said, looking back at the fast-food joint, longing in her eyes, "We didn't get ice cream."

"Ice cream is for good girls only, little mouse," Liam noted the disappointment on her face and expected more of a fuss, but Cammie held her protests.

When they got home, Liam ordered Cammie to grab her things and wait for him in her room. Cammie had opened her mouth as if to argue, then nodded and quietly disappeared into the house.

"Cammie, you know I don't want to punish you."

"I know Daddy."

"But you've been a bad girl."

"Yes, Daddy."

"Please choose your punishment," Liam said, indicating the bedside table where they kept a variety of punishment tools.

"Do I have to, Daddy?"

"Yes, little mouse. Choose." Liam's big form was taking up the space in the doorway, his arms folded, watching Cammie closely. She went to the table and pulled open the drawer. She pulled out the paddle Liam had used on her the first night and set it down on the bed.

"One more," Liam prompted, and Cammie returned to the drawer. She knew which he preferred and pulled it out. It was a thick, silicone, vibrating dildo.

"Good girl, little mouse."
Cammie had chosen to wear clothes that fit slightly looser in order to accommodate the diaper she had been made to wear. Cammie had only kept the diaper on because there was nowhere inconspicuous to discard it while she was removing the butt plug.

"Please take off your work clothes, Cammie," Liam asked, rolling up his sleeves and stepping into the room, closing the door behind him.

Our little girl has been very naughty. Liam texted

Josie.

Naughty girls get punished. Make little Cammie understand. Josie texted back.

Liam set the phone aside and smiled; Cammie was standing in front of him, completely undressed except for the diaper.

"What do you want me to do, Daddy?" Cammie asked, shivering slightly. Liam indicated the chair, and she immediately went to it, waiting for him to sit down.

Liam patted his lap, and Cammie bent over it, her hands resting on the carpet by his feet. Her legs were dangling on the other side, and her ass pointed into the air.

Using his bare hand, he brought it down onto her diapered ass, the sound loud because of the fabric. Cammie squirmed, but it wasn't from pain. Liam spanked her twice more, allowing the sound echo off the walls.

Liam undid the velcro sides of the diaper and folded the back of the diaper away. He could see for sure now that Cammie had removed her butt plug. Liam stroked her bottom slowly. Running his fingers over and down her ass, pressing a thumb to her ass hole, causing Cammie to shiver. He let his fingers continue their path, and he pressed a finger to her pussy lips, feeling her quiver beneath his touch.

Again Liam spanked her ass, this time without the protection of the diaper. Cammie squealed.

"Count."

And she did.

When they reached ten, he stopped and rubbed her ass again, "Stand."

Cammie obeyed, letting the diaper fall free. Without being prompted to, Cammie collected it and placed it on the bedside table.

"Good girl." Liam had the dildo in his hand, delighting in the way her eyes grew wider as she took notice of it in his possession.

Cammie felt the heat pool between her legs. Liam's spanking had stirred the moisture to spread through her pussy, but seeing the hunger in his eyes, her heart thumped violently. Liam would never outright hurt her, but punishment was punishment, and the dildo was *huge.*

She had never had it, or anything close to it, inside her.

"What do we say, Cammie?"

"I'm sorry, Daddy."

"Keep going."

"I'm sorry for taking my butt plug out and lying about it."

"Good, now," Liam pointed to the foot of the bed, and Cammie obeyed. She bent over the edge of the bed and spread her legs, now completely naked to his view.

"You seem to enjoy getting punished, little mouse."

"Yes, Daddy." Cammie hadn't attempted a lie this time, and Liam smiled.

"We're just getting started, Cammie. Lying is a very serious issue."

"Yes, Daddy." Cammie's hand went to her pussy lips, spreading them for Liam. Liam chuckled, "Not yet, little one." Liam placed the dildo in front of her. He wanted Cammie to see what he was about to put into her.

Liam fastened the fuzzy cuffs around her, ankles, "Are they comfortable? Do you remember your safe word?"

"Yes, Daddy." Cammie breathed.

Liam ran the head of the dildo over her pussy lips, letting her moisture coat it. It slid easily over her lips and her ass hole. Cammie stifled a small groan. He pressed the tip of the dildo against her ass hole and pushed. Liam was careful as he slowly worked the head of the dildo into her hole. Cammie moaned, and her body instinctively stiffened, making Liam's effects harder.

"Relax, little one." Liam massaged the cheeks of her ass, spreading them further apart to ease the dildo in further. Cammie clawed at the bed coverings, dragging them closer. She bit into the folds and let out groans and small screams. Tears had gathered in the corners of her eyes, "Daddy, it's too much."

"You know what to do if you want me to

stop, little mouse. You still have to be punished for lying to your Daddy."

Cammie sighed as a wave of pleasure hit her, making the tightness in her ass hole, bearable, "Yes, Daddy."

Liam worked the dildo in as far as it could go. Cammie was panting on the bed, and her pussy was coated in moisture from her pleasure. Her thighs glistened as well.

Liam's cock was as hard as ever, but he maintained control as he touched her swollen clit with his finger. Cammie jerked, the sensation was startling and intense.

"I want to make sure, little mouse, that you never lie to your Daddy again."

"I won't lie again, Daddy, I promise." Cammie's voice was a rough whisper, and her hands were still fisted in the crumpled bedsheets.

"I want to make sure you don't lie to your Mommy again."

"I promise, Daddy, I promise." Cammie was bucking her hips as he massaged her clit.

"Let's make sure, little mouse." Liam pulled away, and Cammie whimpered.

Liam grabbed the paddle from the bed and pressed it against Cammie's ass. Her entire body quivered.

"Count for Daddy, please, little mouse."

Cammie counted, each followed by a hard *whack* from the paddle. Her bottom was burning, and Cammie whimpered for a different reason.

When she reached five, Liam turned the vibrating function of the dildo on. Cammie arched her back and moaned loudly, "Daddy..."

Cammie's voice was faint and broken by panting, but she continued to count for Liam. The blows were softer this time, making the vibration in her ass that much harder to ignore.

Liam set the paddle aside, watching the girl squirm and pant, clutching at the sheets, and biting into the fabric. Her ass hole was being stretched to its fullest by the thick dildo, juices flowing from both her holes.

"Daddy," Cammie half-growled as he

switched the vibrator off. Her hand instantly went to her pussy, trying to ease the burn of desire.

"Cammie, stop," Liam ordered.

Cammie pulled her hand away reluctantly, her pussy clenching and unclenching, causing more juices to flow from it.

"Good girl," Liam kissed the tender, red marks on her ass cheeks and wiggled the dildo, eliciting moans from Cammie as she pressed back against his hand.

"Wait here, little mouse. Don't touch." Liam ordered and left the room.

Cammie lay panting, feeling the stretch of the dildo in her ass, feeling the thick girth of it as it filled her completely. It hurt still, but she was so close to an orgasm. She was tempted. She could just reach down...

Cammie stopped herself. Balling fistfuls of blanket in her hands to keep her from breaking more of the rules.

When Liam returned, Josie was with him, still dressed in her work uniform. She took up the empty chair and watched. Cammie was bound to the bed, her hair messed, and her face flushed. Josie saw the red marks on her bottom from where Liam had been punishing her.

Liam ran his hands over Cammie's ass cheeks again, heat coming off of them. He massaged them, pulling them apart and letting his hands trail down further. Liam stroked the outer lips of Cammie's pussy with his thumbs. His fingers were instantly coated, making them slip more readily into her folds.

Cammie moaned and caught Josie's eye. She was watching intently and unbuttoning the dark blue shirt of her uniform, only stopping to untie her hair. Cammie's pussy twitched.

Liam pushed his thumb deep into her pussy, feeling the heat and moisture, enjoying the way her muscles clamped onto him as her desire burned through her. Again, Liam pulled back, letting Cammie hover on the edge of her orgasm. The look in her eyes was wild, demanding, and her whimper was her plea.

Josie let her shirt fall away, and Cammie was afforded an excellent view of Josie's large breasts, enveloped in a lace bra that barely held onto the weight of them. Even from this distance, Cammie could tell that Josie's nipples were hard. She stood and unbuckled the belt of her pants, letting them slide down her thighs sensually. Liam started pumping the dildo in and out of Cammie's ass, causing her to groan in pleasure. A groan that ended in a growl when Liam stopped, "Daddy, please."

"Please, what, little mouse?" Liam asked

"Please don't stop, Daddy."

"Only good girls get to make demands, little Cammie," Josie said as she stepped out of her pants. Josie was still wearing her heeled boots. She looked intimidatingly beautiful, and Cammie stuffed another fistful of fabric in her mouth to stifle a moan.

Liam turned the vibrator back on and stepped towards Josie.

"Remember, little girl, no touching," Josie

said as Liam pulled her to him and kissed her.

It was hot and demanding, and Josie could feel his cock pressed against her, hard and throbbing. Her body responded to him instantly. Liam kissed her neck and slid his hands into her panties, stroking her. Josie threw her head back and sighed with pleasure, "Yes, Liam."

Liam inserted his fingers into her waiting pussy and stroked her slowly, licking her neck and breathing heavily into her ear. Josie moaned, and Cammie moaned in response to their play. Josie unzipped Liam's trousers and freed his cock. It was hard and throbbing and hot as she wrapped her hands around his shaft, stroking him as he fingered her. With Cammie watching them, her body tingled and burst into flame.

Her pussy demanded his cock, but she knew Cammie's punishment would come first.

Cammie moaned again, bucking, trying to push the dildo deeper into her ass hole, attempting in vain to ease the ache in her pussy, "Mommy? Daddy? Please?"

Cammie was whimpering, and Liam's cock twitched again. "Go to her, Liam." Josie said breathlessly, "Show Cammie what happens to little girls who lie."

Liam kissed Josie, hard, pushing his fingers deeper into her wet hole, feeling her body clamp down as she came close to orgasming. He pulled away, a little reluctantly, and went to Cammie. Again, he stopped the vibrator, and the moan that escaped Cammie's lips was one of frustration and pure desire.

"Daddy," Cammie pushed herself up on her elbows, her pussy twitching and her body shivering from unspent need, "Daddy, please."

Liam knelt in front of Cammie, his cock at attention, thick, throbbing, and hot. Without asking for permission, Cammie wrapped her small fingers around his cock, her eyes dark with lust, and put her mouth around his head, flicking her tongue over it as Jose had demonstrated.

Liam's eyes closed involuntarily, and a deep sigh of pleasure escaped his body, causing his cock to twitch violently and release beads of precum as his little girl continued pleasuring him. When Liam opened his eyes, he saw Josie standing behind Cammie, a grin on her face, "Our little girl is enjoying herself, Liam."

"She's soaked and dripping." Josie said, thickly, "Her pussy is twitching."

Liam groaned in response to Josie's words. She was making it harder for him to maintain control. He didn't want to cum yet.

Cammie opened her mouth wider and took his whole cock, slurping and massaging him with her tongue. She was a fast learner.

"You're getting good at that, little mouse." Liam's voice was hoarse, and Cammie moaned the second Josie touched the tip of her tongue to her swollen lips.

The vibration of Cammie's moan, combined with the view of his wife licking Cammie's pussy, was nearly enough to make him lose control. He pulled away, shaking. Liam met Josie's gaze and saw the mischief in her eyes. She knew how to push him.

Cammie moaned again as Josie slipped a finger into her pussy, stroking her.

Liam sank to his knees in front of Josie and spread her legs. As Josie adjusted for Liam, she pushed another finger into Cammie's soaking pussy. Then another. The girl's entire body quivered, right on the edge of her orgasm. Josie pulled away, again denying Cammie release.

"Promise us, Cammie, that you will never lie again. No matter what."

"I promise, Mommy." Liam's tongue slid between Josie's pussy lips, and a moan escaped.

Cammie repeated herself, again and again. She meant it, and with every word, Cammie seemed to be struggling to control her tears, "From the bottom of my heart, Mommy. I promise."

"Good girl, Cammie." With that, Josie wiggled the dildo, then proceeded to fuck her small hole with the large object. Cammie moaned, louder than before, and pushed back against Josie's hands as her fingers found her wet pussy again.

Cammie's body was flushed, glistening with pleasure and sweat. She couldn't take the torment any longer. She pushed back against Josie's hands, attempting to increase the pressure that Josie was exerting. It was no use. Josie pulled away again, and Cammie was left panting, crying, and pleading. Josie could feel her own body twitch and convulse as she came closer and closer to that edge. She could understand the complete madness that Cammie felt as her orgasm kept being denied. Liam pulled away from Josie, and she immediately went to Cammie's other side. Josie lay in front of Cammie and spread her legs open for the girl, baring herself to her. Josie was wet from her own juices and Liam's tongue.

Cammie stared and licked her lips, "Can I touch you, Mommy?"

"Yes, sweet girl."

Cammie gingerly ran her finger through the folds of Josie's pussy. Her skin was soft, and the juices were sticky. Her scent was driving Cammie mad, so she pressed her lips to Josie's pussy and pushed her tongue into her hole.

Josie rested her head back as Cammie's tongue lapped at her clit, then circled it, varying the pressure, "Good girl, Cammie."

Liam pressed his cock against Cammie's waiting pussy, it twitched. He gripped his cock in his fist and ran it across her wet lips, coating it as he had done with the dildo. It took less time than it did before.

From his vantage point, Liam could see Josie's pussy on display for their little girl. She was obediently licking and sucking on Josie's clit, her body responding to the scent and taste of her Mommy by becoming wetter, and her hips grinding in the air, begging for release. Cammie pushed back against Liam's cock.

As a matter to get himself under control so he wouldn't cum the second he entered her, Liam stroked her pussy with the head of his cock and pumped the dildo in and out of her ass. It was still there, filling Cammie's small hole, stretching it as far as it could go. Cammie had gotten used to it and was pushing back in time with his play. Both Josie and Cammie moaned in unison. Josie, from Cammie's continuous suckling, and Cammie from Liam's play.

Liam's cock burned with need. He felt his desire build up in his belly. Slowly, Liam pushed his cock into Cammie's waiting pussy. It gripped his cock tightly, twitching and clamping down on him as he entered her. The dildo in her ass was taking up enough space that he could feel it pressing against his own cock as he slowly slid in and out of Cammie's pussy.

The girl moaned, then whimpered, "Yes, Daddy, please, fuck me." Instead of scolding her, Liam thrust his cock balls deep into her. He wanted Cammie to feel his every thrust as he entered her; he wanted the girl to understand that punishment and reward could be doled out as he saw fit. Cammie had inserted her entire hand into Josie's pussy, pushing her fist in and out of her, causing thick globs of sticky fluid to smear over her arm and drip onto the bed.

Josie's moans were becoming louder, and Cammie's body was responding to them.

Liam gripped Cammie's hips and pulled out just far enough that just the head of his cock remained inside of her. Even with the large amount of lubrication, the girl's pussy was so tight that it took effort not to pound her into sweet oblivion.

"Cammie?"

"Yes, Daddy?" She was breathless and shaking.

"Do you want to cum?"

"Yes, please, Daddy. Make me cum."

Josie's own scream of pleasure caused Cammie's pussy to twitch a few times. "Please, Daddy," she repeated again, a crack in her voice.

Liam leaned over her, still only keeping the head of his cock in her hole, "Alright, little mouse. Ask me again, and mean it."

"Please," Cammie whimpered, her voice was thick, and she begged Liam, "Please, please make me cum, Daddy."

"Again." Liam thrust in slowly, feeling her

pussy contract around him.

"Make me cum on your cock, Daddy. Pretty please, Daddy. I need to cum." Cammie's pleas were sweet and satisfying as he increased his speed. Cammie no longer bothered muffling her moans and screams. He pounded his cock into Cammie, pushing harder and stroking faster. Liam gripped her hips tightly and thrust into her, feeling his orgasm peak just as she screamed her final release.

Cammie's body twitched and convulsed around his cock, drawing him closer to the edge before her second orgasm ripped through her. Her small body clenched so hard he gave a guttural growl as his cock shot ropes of cum into her pussy, over and over again.

Cammie's breaths came in gasps. Her body was shaking and shivering, convulsing around his cock, slowly causing the dildo to push itself out. Liam switched it on and held it in place. The vibrations shot through her, causing her to scream once more. Cammie's body clamped down on his cock, hard, and he groaned from the pleasure of it.

When Liam's cock stopped twitching, he slipped it out of Cammie's filled pussy, watching as cum dripped out, running down her thighs and onto the bed.

Liam's cock was still hard, and he stroked it slowly, coating his hand in their juices. He felt a second orgasm building, and he pumped his cock hard and fast, shooting more cum over Cammie's ass and back.

Liam stood panting, enjoying the view that lay before him. Cammie was covered in his cum and her own fluids. The vibrator was still sticking out of her ass, causing Cammie to moan continuously, thrashing her head from side to side. Josie lay in front of Cammie, the girl's fist still inside Josie's pussy. By the look on Josie's face, Cammie was clenching and unclenching her fists. Cammie's trembling was causing her a great deal of pleasure. Cammie let out a long, deep moan as Liam slowly pulled the dildo free from her ass. With a sigh, the girl collapsed, her body trembling.

"Cammie," Josie called, "one more time, little one. Please make Mommy cum."

Cammie obeyed, her hair damp and her body glittering from their play. Her fist was still inside Josie's pussy, and soon Cammie's tongue was working on her clit.

Liam left the two on the bed, and he snuck out of the room for a shower.

Chapter 11

Cammie had been awaiting this day for the last thirty days, and it was about time it got here. While she had grown to enjoy some things about her community service, it was certainly not something she wanted to keep doing. She was grateful that her sentence had been light.

Today also marked her thirty days sober. She had attended the court-mandated meetings and had found that she genuinely benefited from them and decided that she would continue the meetings.

The agency assured her that the hours and everything else required by the court would be handed over properly.

Cammie found that the time spent serving the community sometimes allowed her to learn new things about herself. As an example, Cammie knew that she *hated* cooking. She had spent time both serving the food as well as making it at the soup kitchen she was assigned to. It was too much stress. What she did love, however, was talking with the old people at the retirement village. Cammie intended to continue helping out even after her service ended.

As usual, Liam had offered to drive Cammie wherever she needed to go. Cammie had managed to get her car from the police impound lot a week ago but had fallen into a relaxed kind of routine with them.

Today, however, Cammie had asked Liam if she could drive herself.

"I thought you liked it when I drove you around, little mouse."

"I do, Daddy," Cammie giggled, "but I think I should at least drive myself on my last day." When Liam just looked at her, Cammie continued, "So I can show you and Mommy that I've learned my lesson."

"Have you learned your lesson, Cammie?"

"Yes, Daddy." Cammie had such a serious look on her face that Liam could not help but chuckle.

"If you are sure, little mouse."

Cammie nodded enthusiastically, smiling broadly.

Cammie greeted the people she had come to know over the last thirty days warmly. They were all celebrating their last day today, which meant the atmosphere was supercharged with excitement and joy.

The last day was also the hardest that their supervisor had scheduled. It was nearly a hundred degrees out today. They were working the last quarter-mile stretch on the road out of town, so not too many cars came through this early in the day. Still, even in the sweltering heat, their morale did not falter.

They joked, laughed, danced, and miraculously, worked faster than they had in any previous assignment on this particular stretch of road.

Weeds were pulled up, trash was collected, and sharp objects disposed of.

Cammie was cheerful, even as sweat ran down her

back and into the diaper she was still wearing. It was mildly uncomfortable, but Liam had promised that if she continued being a good girl, she got to take it off and only wear it at night.

Cammie had all but skipped to her car that afternoon, her heart lighter than it had been since the month had started. Her first stop was Liam and Josie's home.

My home, too. Cammie corrected. Cammie loved living with them. She was happier and healthier than she had ever been in her life.

Cammie stripped out of her overalls that they had bought specifically for the community service. It had made her feel more secure that no one could see her diaper when she wore the overalls.

Cammie stuffed her dirty clothes in the hamper and discarded the sweaty diaper in the bin next to it. She ran to the shower naked, giggling as she went. She was home alone but still felt giddy at the thought of being caught naked.

She washed the heat of the day from her body, loving the way the water flowed over her. The soft caress reminded her of Liam and Josie's touches, and her body tingled in response. Cammie wanted to touch herself but held off.

She was better at following the rules, now, too. She dried off, replaced the diaper, and got dressed.

The real reason for Cammie wanting to drive herself was that she wanted to get Liam and Josie a few small things to say thank you.

At the start of all of this, she had acted like a complete brat. *More than what was called for, to be sure,* Cammie thought. They had taught her that there was more than one way to deal with messy emotions.

Not only that, Liam and Josie had taken her in and cared for her. Despite her nearly losing her job and her apartment. Cammie had managed to get through her near-miss relatively unscathed.

***

"Mommy? Daddy?" Cammie began.

Liam and Josie sat side by side on the couch and

waited. Cammie had texted them and asked them to meet her in the living room as soon as they got home.

"I want to say something, and it's very important."

"Go on, little mouse." Liam encouraged.

"When we met, I was-" Cammie paused to try to find the words, "everything was a big mess." Cammie knelt in front of them and took both Liam and Josie's hands into her own and held on to them.

"You taught me that messes can be cleaned up."
Liam and Josie exchanged a look and then looked back at Cammie.

"What is this about, sweetheart?" Josie asked, rubbing her thumb over the back of Cammie's hand wrapped around hers.
Cammie's face flushed, but she didn't waver, "I got you guys something today."

"Is that why you were so secretive this morning?" Liam asked, a frown wrinkling his forehead.

Cammie nodded, her face turning redder, "I wanted it to be a surprise."

"Alright, alright! Don't keep us waiting." Josie laughed and shooed Cammie.

A short minute later, Cammie returned, struggling with a big gift bag.

Liam got up and offered her a hand, to which Cammie stuck her tongue out at, "No, I can do this, Daddy."

Liam chuckled and returned to his seat, "Alright, little mouse, we can do this your way."

Cammie, satisfied, plopped the bag down in front of them and reached inside.

"This one is for Daddy," she said and handed him a carefully wrapped object. "And this one is for Mommy," Cammie said and handed her a similar looking package. Liam opened his and stared at it. It must have been the biggest mug he had ever seen. He turned it over.

"Best Daddy in the world?" Liam's voice had a hint of laughter, but he managed to suppress it, "I love it, little mouse."

Josie unwrapped hers, and it had the same basic sentiment on it.

Cammie looked excitedly at Josie, "They also change color when you add hot water."

Josie stood and dutifully turned the kettle on and waited for it to boil. She poured the water into the mug and watched as the black mug turned white.

Josie's eyes grew wider in surprise, "Cammie!"

Cammie giggled.

"What is it, Jo?" Liam asked, an amused smile still on his lips.

Josie returned to her seat to show them. Instead of "Best Mommy in the World," a large, pink pussy replaced it.

Liam's eyes flickered to the bag, "Did you go to the naughty store?"

Cammie's eyes glittered, and her face turned a shade redder, "Maybe."

Cammie pulled out a large wooden paddle and handed it to her Daddy.

When the gifts had been doled out, Cammie threw

her arms around Josie, "I promise I won't be that bad ever again, Mommy."

"I have one more present," Cammie said as she stood and unbuttoned her blouse. She didn't take it off yet, wanting to make a show of it. The lady at the store had helped her get into it.

Cammie unbuttoned her jeans and very slowly slid it down her lean legs and kicked it off. The blouse afforded enough cover that only the barest of hints of flesh was shown. Cammie hadn't asked for permission to go without her diaper, but she had had to make a choice. The harness and diaper wouldn't both fit under her clothes, and the diaper would ruin the visual she was going for, so she had removed it.

There was one more thing that she had gotten for herself while she was out shopping. As her jeans slid down, a furry tail popped free. Cammie bit her lower lip as Liam and Josie looked on in awe.

Cammie turned around and wiggled her bottom at them, her blouse covering most of her ass, but the tail hanging freely.

She heard Liam suck in a breath, and her body started tingling. She expected that she would be punished for not wearing the diaper, but for now, Cammie was basking in the rapt attention from Liam and Josie.

Cammie turned to face them. She was shaking a little, her nerves were on fire, and her body tingled and burned in response.

Then she made a show of walking to the bag and pulling out the matching headpiece that came with the tail. Cammie bent low, exposing her ass to Liam and Josie. The tail was blocking a full view of her already moist pussy lips, but the effect was what she had intended.

Cammie's heart was racing as she turned her back on them again. Liam and Josie were quiet but had not once taken their eyes off of her. Cammie was mesmerizing.

"Are you guys ready?" Cammie asked innocently.

"Ready for?" Josie asked, her eyes still looking at the way the tail swayed back and forth as Cammie moved.

"Your final present," Cammie said and lifted the hem of her blouse, revealing the straps of the gray leather harness. The leather was tight against her skin, and the buckles hot from her body heat. Cammie lowered the blouse from her shoulders, slowly inching it down, exposing her back. There were no straps there, just bare, silky flesh that glowed under the bright lights.

"There was just one more way I could show you how much you mean to me," Cammie said, "Only one way to show how happy my Mommy and Daddy have made me."

Cammie dropped the blouse to the ground, completely naked now except for the harness. Cammie wiggled her ass again, making the tail waggle back and forth. She dropped to her knees and looked over her shoulder at them. Cammie grabbed the end of the tail in her hand and stuck the end of it in her mouth, suckling on it.

Josie saw that the tail was a butt plug and not attached to the harness. Josie licked her lips, and

Liam cleared his throat, "Cammie."

"I want you and Mommy to teach me how to be naughty." Cammie looked at them, her eyes dark, and spread her legs a little, exposing her most sensitive parts to the air and light. A shiver ran down her spine.

"Little mouse," Liam started but couldn't quite tell her no.

"Please, Daddy?" Cammie stretched her arms out in front of her, arching her back. Cammie rose to her feet slowly and faced them. The harness was tied around her throat, and straps ran down the front of her, between her breasts and tight against her skin.

The straps of the harness came together at her hips, where another strap encircled them. More straps ran from her hips down to her thighs. There were metal loops for ropes, clips, and other straps. Something Cammie had insisted upon.

"Do you like it?" Cammie asked, uncertain, as she twirled around for them again.

"I love it, little mouse, Liam said.

"Did you pick it out yourself?" Josie asked and circled Cammie.

"I did, Mommy. I thought of what you might like, and the lady helped me."

Cammie swayed her hips, swinging the end of the tail in her hands and made herself comfortable on Josie's lap. Josie was stunned. Their meek little mouse had turned slightly wild.

"Please, Mommy? I really want to show you that I have learned my lesson." Cammie nuzzled Josie's neck, planting soft kisses along her jaw and behind her ear.

Josie pressed herself against Cammie's back, feeling her heat seep through her clothes, "Well, then, little one, we should put it to good use."

Cammie jumped in surprise as Josie's fingers touched her moist pussy lips, and she threw her head back against Josie's shoulder. Josie expertly drew moans from Cammie's lips as Liam watched.

"What happens when you break the rules, little mouse?"

"I get punished."

"That's right."

"What happens if you are a good girl?" With that, Josie pulled her hand away, and Cammie knew she wasn't about to have her way just yet.

"On your knees, little girl," Josie demanded. Cammie obeyed instantly, her eyes glossing over just a little as she felt the tail being tugged as she dropped to her knees. Josie had the tip in her hands and was rhythmically tugging on it. The sensation rippled through Cammie, and her pussy twitched.

Liam approached her, a leather leash in his hands. The one that came with the harness. He clipped the leash to the metal ring at her neck and pulled the slack tight.

"Daddy?"

"Yes, little mouse?"

"Are you mad at me? I only wanted to do something special for you." Cammie's voice was soft, and her eyes were staring up at him, trusting and a little scared.

"No, little one. We're not angry." Josie said

and stroked her hair.

"Mommy's right," Liam said, smiling down at her, "but you know the rules, little mouse. You weren't allowed to take your diaper off until we got home."

"I know, Daddy."

Liam dropped to his knees in front of her, pulling her face up to his and kissed the tip of her nose, "Your punishment will be over before you even know it."

"Okay, Daddy." Cammie smiled relieved.

"Good girl."

"Now, open your mouth, little mouse," Liam commanded as he unzipped his pants. Cammie licked her lips, unable to hide her desire and did as she was told.

The leather leash was pulled tighter, forcing Cammie closer to his hard cock. Cammie gripped his cock and held it steady, slowly running her tongue around the swollen head.

"No, Cammie, no teasing."

Cammie stopped and opened her mouth wide.

Liam thrust his throbbing cock into her waiting mouth and pulled the leash tighter. There was very little for Cammie to do except take his cock as deep as she could. Cammie sucked his cock into her throat, feeling it fill her up. She gagged, and Liam pulled out slightly, giving her a moment to breathe. She nodded, and Liam pushed deeper, feeling his hardness slide deep into her throat. Cammie knew she had to relax or she would choke again. Tears were forming in the corners of her eyes as Liam thrust a slow rhythm.

Josie joined Cammie on the floor, running her hands over Cammie's body, pinching her nipples and delighting in the muffled moans coming from her. Josie reached around and ran her fingers through Cammie's pussy lips, coating her fingers in her moisture.

Josie licked her lips and looked up at Liam, her eyes meeting his. There was a lot of heat and desire in them, but also love.

"Cammie," Josie whispered in her ear, flicking a fingertip over Cammie's nipple.

Cammie whined softly, unable to respond verbally. Josie increased her strokes in Cammie's pussy, feeling her body clutch at her fingers as her pleasure built.

"Cum for Mommy, little girl," Josie commanded.

Liam thrust his cock deep into Cammie's throat, watching as the girl's body shivered and twitched under Josie's intense touch. Cammie's body clenched around Josie's fingers, begging for more. Cammie swallowed his cock as far as it could go, feeling his hardness twitch as she did so. Her orgasm flooded through her, eliciting deep moans of pleasure.

Liam groaned loudly as he orgasmed, cum filling up Cammie's little mouth. He pulled back slightly and let some slack out of the leash, cum leaking from the corners of her mouth.

When his cock stopped twitching, and he pulled out of her mouth. Cammie continued licking and cleaning cum from his cock, suckling and enjoying the grunts she could draw from him with that small act.

"Good girl, little mouse."

Cammie panted, moans filling the room, and leaned back into Josie's warm body, her fingers drawing Cammie's orgasm out. She twitched and shivered.

"Do you want more, little girl?"

"Yes, Mommy," Cammie whispered, delirious.

"What do we say?"

"Please, Mommy."

"That's a good girl," Josie said and pinched Cammie's nipple, hard. Cammie moaned louder, pressing herself against Josie as her fingers continued teasing her nipples and her pussy.

"Jo, let's give this good little girl the treat she wants," Liam said and pulled on the leash. Cammie reluctantly pulled away from Josie's teasing touch and stood. Cammie's legs were slightly unsteady as she walked behind Liam, led by the leash to Liam and Josie's room.

Who is Tina Moore?

Tina Moore has enjoyed the lifestyle of a Mommy Domme for several years. She began exploring kink and BDSM in her youth and found her love of being a strict Mommy Domme in early 2000. Tina Moore is now an author of many MDLG, DDLG and ABDL themed novels.

Follow her on:

Author Page on Amazon

Instagram @tinamoore.kdp

If you enjoyed this book, it would be much appreciated if you leave a review.